THE ANGEL CARVER

RANDOM HOUSE

NEW YORK

Rosanne Daryl Thomas

THE ANGEL CARVER

Library of Congress Cataloging-in-Publication Data
Thomas, Rosanne Daryl.
The angel carver / by Rosanne Daryl Thomas
p.   cm.
ISBN 0–679–42363–X
I. Title.
PS3566.R575A83   1993   813′ .54—dc20   92-37032

Manufactured in the United States of America
Book design by J. K. Lambert
24689753
First Edition

FOR
Lisa Mann

THE ANGEL CARVER

THE ANGEL CARVER

Consensus is, he had to be guilty of something. Guilty, crazy or a fool. If it was not the crime of which he was accused, if it wasn't murder, then perhaps some other crime, some secret crime known only to himself and one other? What else is there to make of him? Of her? Of the jewel-eyed angels?

It is not enough to say, There stands an empty storefront. It is not enough to say that Reliable Repair can no longer be relied upon, that the shoe man is gone. And so they speculate, the reporters, the cops, the neighbors, the collectors, but what they say reveals more about their own lust, greed and suspicion than about the Angel Carver.

What do they *know?*

Much less than I will tell you.

Reliable Repair had always been where it now stands empty, and the shoe man had always been at his bench in the window, as long as always is, as long as local memory.

The shoe man had occupied the shop, an underheated cavern of mint-painted tin on the corner of Flatbush and Parker, for so long that the rent had risen from thirty-five dollars a month to eight hundred. He stood in his window, wrapped in his cardigan, tapping and gluing, looking up now and then, smiling at the passersby if the passersby smiled first.

Like an angel, the shoe man was invisible until the moment he was needed. Then there he was, to fix your heel, resole your favorite shoes, save you the ever increasing expense of buying new. And then he disappeared, from your thoughts at least, until he was needed again. He wasn't a man whose name was known. If he was called at all, he was called the shoe man. And he liked it that way.

To say the shoe man valued his anonymity is to misunderstand. It was so much a part of him, it was beyond his notice. Do you value your tongue? You don't even think about your tongue unless it is bloody, burnt or blistered. The shoe man didn't think about his privacy until he lost it. And even after all that happened, it was easier for most of the folks in the neighborhood to remember the dust on the window than his face behind the glass.

No one knew nor would have cared to guess that this same man was the Angel Carver. Regardless of what you may have heard, that is a fact.

At the age when young men should be thinking about that sort of thing, the shoe man hadn't inclined toward one trade or another. It was just luck that one of the Italians who really knew the business the way it used to be done had no sons of his own. And luck that the shoe man happened along. Before then, he had had no idea what his own hands could do. The old man's tools were like extensions of the young man's fingers. It was as if these tools had been waiting for these hands and no others. Awed by his apprentice's gift, the old man retired to Florida, feeling blessed. It was an honor to leave the tools that had been his life in hands such as these, an honor.

The shoe man took his savings and the tools that were now his and opened Reliable Repair. Next to a subway and a newsstand and a coffee shop, it was a good location, the best. He borrowed to have his name painted on the window in big gold letters. JACK STANDINI. That was all he wanted. That, and a wife.

He was handsome then and being that in those days people were less inclined to throw their old shoes in the trash, lots of pretty girls came into the shop. The prettiest was Angela. He fell in love and married her and they moved to an apartment walking distance from work. They spent their wedding money on a red-topped kitchen table with shiny silver legs and four matching chairs and a double bed. Though she never saw it, the first angel he carved was for her. An angel for Angela.

In those happiest of days, when he closed the shop for an hour at noon, his Angela would have lunch waiting and they'd eat quickly so there was time to make love and get back to the shop before one. They wanted a baby right away, a little one with her thick hair and his dark eyes and her laugh and his tenderness and her long legs and his strong hands and so on.

Sometimes Angela went into Manhattan alone. She'd visit her aunt or look for bargains on Fourteenth Street. If he was home when she was gone, he'd work on her angel. It was a simple one, a bow-lipped baby face with two small wings on either side carved from a block. And it was meant to be a surprise.

One Sunday afternoon after they'd made love and gone for a walk in Prospect Park, Angela decided to go to Orchard Street. She needed a new foundation. The shoe man said he'd go with her. She laughed and kissed his eyebrows. "What do you know about women's underwear?" she asked him. He walked her to the subway, the same subway that is still there today, and went home to work on her angel. That was in 1952.

Looking back, he remembered the train rumbling into the

underground station, the way his kiss just missed her mouth as she grabbed the rail and tapped down the stairs in her high-heeled ankle boots with the furry top trim, the way her plaid coat billowed behind her and she raised one arm to wave without looking back. She didn't come home that night or ever again.

It wasn't that she had died suddenly or been murdered or kidnapped. Any one of those things, as awful as they were, would have done for an explanation. There was no explanation. For years the police kept an eye out, but they didn't have evidence that she was dead. They didn't have evidence that she was alive. She never filed for divorce or sent for her grandmother's gold locket. There might have been another man but if there was he didn't know who it might have been or why she wouldn't have asked for her freedom. He walked every street in Manhattan searching for her face, and tormented himself with the thought that while he walked across Fifty-third, she might be walking down Seventh. Her face was posted in police stations. No woman matching her description was reported seen in the city or elsewhere in the United States. She was just gone. Not like a soldier shot down over Korea or captured by the reds, not like those poor boys who disappeared into the Vietnam jungle or the yellow Arabian desert. She was lost, like a glove or a sock or a dream, missing. For years, the shoe man hoped that on the day he lost her, she had lost herself and that one day, when she found herself and her memory of their love, she would come home. But there was no evidence that she had lost her memory. Or that she hadn't.

The shoe man waited. He had his memories, brief as they were. As he waited, he finished carving the bow-lipped angel, painted the face in Angela's colors and hung it on the wall in the back room near the window overlooking the neighbor's yard. Then he started another.

Time passed. As his face grew older, Angela's stayed nineteen. In his mind, Angela never aged a day past the day he lost her. Still, he wondered if somewhere in the world he had a son or daughter reaching middle age. He listed the telephone in the directory exactly as it had been listed in 1952. He kept the apartment they had known together so that if Angela came looking, she would find. If she came up the subway steps, she would see Reliable Repair and he would be in the window.

After a point, he had more angels than hopes of holding Angela in his arms again. Still, he couldn't bring himself to have his wife declared legally dead. He couldn't remarry and he didn't want to start with a new wife. Impossible. There were women, nice enough ones, who didn't want to be wives. He'd gone dancing once with one of these and come back to the double bed alone and feeling untrue. And there were women he could pay to hold and lie with. That felt worse.

He had his hands and his angels. What his hands could do

with leather was nothing compared to what they could do with good wood. He tested himself. If he pictured a wind-bent wing, he could carve it. If he wanted to seize the divine instant when a guardian angel shielded his charge, it was within his power. Working on his angels brought him a soaring ecstasy. And the more he gave himself to them, the less his soul yearned for womanly comfort. Funny thing—he didn't quite believe in God, and yet he surrounded himself with seraphim, cherubim, the many-eyed chariots, domin-ions, virtues and powers, archangels, angels, principalities, all of whom he'd carved himself, all of whom he'd painted and adorned. He believed in them. And in the absorbing night hours while he brought their features to within a shade of life, their wings a feather away from flight, they rewarded him with forgetfulness.

There was no cure for the morning hours, when the ones with somewhere else to go marched in a multicolored column down the cement stairs to the subway. There was no cure for the afternoon, when, in spite of the odds and plain common sense, he searched the tired faces that passed his window.

One morning, before he left for the shop, the shoe man sat in his back room among his angels. As he looked out on the garden in his neighbor's yard, a full-grown parrot appeared on the branches of Mrs. Rice's oak. He knew the parrot did not belong to her. He coaxed the red, blue, yellow, green bird to the sill of his back room window with toast. He decided it was female and called her Angie.

Angie ate pizza when he ate pizza. Angie ate Chinese when he ate Chinese. Angie sat on his shoulder at the red-topped table. Angie rode his shoulder as he walked to work and talked to him during the day. Chattering on her perch in the window, screeching at pedestrians, flapping her wings at the

traffic, she was the next best thing to a wife. And she at-
tracted business.

Angie watched as the shoe man struggled with an especially elaborate gathering of seraphim. Her wings were their
wings and she seemed to know when to spread them as he
worked his way through the four four-headed six-winged
angels, one for the north, south, east and west winds, angels
of love, light and fire that demanded every skill he had
mastered. She accompanied him to Williamsburg, where he
haggled with a Hasid over eight matched and flawless red
rubies. Angie lived to see the shoe man mount the ruby-eyed
seraphim in such a way that when the sun entered the back
room in the early morning, the eyes of the seraphim lit with
fire. Then the parrot died.

He could not bear the loss of his longtime companion. He
took Angie to a taxidermist in Far Rockaway. The taxidermist matched the glass eyes to the shoe man's precise description of Angie's lively eyes. He tilted Angie's head at an
inquisitive angle and spread her feathers coquettishly. She
was so lifelike all she lacked was life. The shoe man hung
Angie on her perch above his bench in the window of the
shop. The stuffed bird didn't do much to ease his grief, but
it reminded him of her, and that was something.

ld Mrs. Rice had eyes good enough to garden. Because the shoe man was in trade, Mrs. Rice never spoke directly to him about more than the splendor or the fault of the day's weather, yet, over many years the shoe man became fond of her and she of him. From his window, he would watch her hired woman, Leopoldine, lower her onto the cushion that protected her ancient knees from the hard soil. Leopoldine would shade her employer's head with a ruffled parasol as she pruned her roses and trained them over a low, arched trellis.

Neither Leopoldine nor the shoe man could understand how she could see well enough to pick aphids off the leaves of her brilliant azaleas and yet never realize that the parrot in the window of Reliable Repair was dead and dusty. Mrs. Rice would stand on the sidewalk in her weighty blonde mink coat murmuring, "Pretty bird," and wiggling her fingers near the glass while Leopoldine went inside the shop.

The only thing that changed with every visit was the weather and the way she wore her coat. If it was spring, her mink hung open. In winter and fall it was buttoned up to her fragile white ears. Mrs. Rice wore her mink the way Atlas wore the globe. Like the globe, it grew tattier with age. But her shoes, the shoes she had Leopoldine bring in for repair, never wore out. The shoe man gave up saying that they didn't need work. Whenever Mrs. Rice wanted her shoes repaired, Leopoldine helped her into her coat and took her on a stroll to the corner. The shoe man figured that the walk was probably the point, but to justify the money he was paid, he did what little he could find to do. There was never a scuffed toe, never a black mark marring the heel, never a ground-down sole that needed rebuilding.

"She walks on air," he'd tell Leopoldine.

Leopoldine would laugh and say, "She leans on me. Look at my shoes."

Not a week after the last time he saw Mrs. Rice waving her fingers at his window, not a week before Lucille appeared, he happened to be thinking of his wife. Not thinking any particular thought, just accidentally about her the way he sometimes did when he was working on his angels. Only he was at his bench in the shop, where memory of Angela refused to visit, had not crossed the threshold for maybe twenty years. He was at his bench gluing new black leather linings into Mrs. Rice's tan kid walking shoes and he looked up in surprise. On the sidewalk he saw Gloria the pizza lady holding a slice with one floury hand as she patted the dark coat of a heavy black woman with the other. The woman lifted her head from Gloria's shoulder to take the slice. It was Leopoldine. The shoe man heard her say she didn't know how she could possibly eat, and he knew.

"Poor Mrs. Rice," said the shoe man. "And these are her shoes in my hand." He caressed the aged but barely worn leather. Leopoldine looked toward the parrot and began to heave and sob all over again. Gloria tried to dust a hand print of white flour off Leopoldine's coat with her floury hand. "I gotta get back," she said, helplessly patting at the worsening mess. "The Albanians."

The bells on the knob jingled frantically as Leopoldine let the shoe man's door slam behind her. She filled the shop with the smell of garlic, hot cheese and tomato. Her rheumy eyes were bloodshot. Tears spilled over the swollen rims of her lids. The shoe man led her to his quick heel repair chair and pulled a smudged chamois cloth out of his pocket. Leopoldine sat and ate and sniffled. He let her be. The closeness of the air, the narrow depth and darkness of Reliable Repair, the comfortable smell of shoe leather and polish seemed to loosen the emotions of certain customers. Over the years, lonely women had wept in that chair. Well-dressed men had confessed unashamedly. If a customer wanted to talk, he listened. He tapped and polished and glued and cut, shaking his head at their sorrows. His customers would take from that what they needed. It seemed to be enough for them that he was there just the same as he had always been there.

As Leopoldine finished her slice, the shoe man waxed the leather of Mrs. Rice's tan shoes until it felt soft, like a woman's hand on his cheek. Leopoldine wiped her purple lips. "You know she had five husbands, that old woman?"

"No." The shoe man knew almost nothing about his former neighbor and he knew more about her than any of the people who lived on the block. He knew she gardened. He'd seen the formal foyer of her house.

"She was widowed at thirty-five. No babies, and she had a pretty little figure on her. I came in at the second man. Wednesdays, for half a day. When he died there was some money, and the third one didn't like me, but she kept me on, Lord rest her . . ."

Mrs. Rice would need nice shoes for the burial. The shoe man blackened the soles and began to pay closer attention.

"He ran off like I knew he would, but the fourth man, he had me in Wednesdays, Fridays, and cooking some nights. He passed out of this world like the others, but he had a good policy and left her provided. Then I moved in."

The shoe man tried to picture Mrs. Rice as an alluring widow. Impossible.

"An' after all them husbands, she married one more time. Liked to have someone to please. Now she's dead."

The shoe man tried to picture his lost Angela as she once was. Impossible.

"You could have been number six, I swear." That was a lie. "If you'd been a little bit bold. Took her in your arms." Just about every time they'd gone to the corner, Mrs. Rice would run her vivid tongue over her chalky lips and say, *That's* what I call masculine without the huff and puff. She'd whisper up close to Leopoldine's ear as if someone might be scandalized by her utterances. Thank the Lord, she'd say, that he's not colored or you would have married right up and left me alone with those wicked, wicked workaday husbands of mine. Don't you dare deny it. Leopoldine never denied it. "She had an eye for you."

"She didn't have no eyes for me, Leopoldine. That woman couldn't tell the difference between dead and alive."

Leopoldine dropped her mourning and laughed. "She gonna be damn surprised to meet up with that parrot in heaven. She sure ain't gon' be seein' her family now or in the evermore." Leopoldine told the shoe man how in the past two days, Mrs. Rice not even in the ground, a swarm of never before seen nieces and nephews had arrived at the house and stripped it. "They took an' tooked," she said. Mrs.

Rice's cherry wood china cupboard, her needlepoint dining room chairs from her mama, the black walnut secretary with the gold trim, all gone. "Even her bed." The shoe man shook his head.

Leopoldine examined the reversed gold and black letters painted in the shoe man's window. All these years she'd never needed to know the shoe man's name. She knew where he was and she knew he'd always be there when she walked through the door with Mrs. Rice's shoes in hand. With Mrs. Rice gone, without Mrs. Rice's shoes, things changed. The paint was too worn to read. "You ought to repaint your sign." Leopoldine wrapped her battered Red Crosses around the legs of his chair. It was too late to ask.

The shoe man saw the rips and holes in Leopoldine's rubber soles. He walked back into the shadows and pulled an unclaimed pair of low-heeled black patent pumps off a shelf. "Been here over a year. Very good leather." He borrowed back his chamois and wiped the dust away, putting the pumps in beside Mrs. Rice's shoes in a used plastic grocery bag.

"I don't know how to thank you," said Leopoldine. Then she had an idea. "I still got keys." She invited him to help himself to what little was left for the taking in Mrs. Rice's brownstone before the lawyers arrived to do whatever the nieces and nephews thought ought to be done.

He declined the invitation. "I have about all I can use."

Leopoldine insisted he come. He wanted to get home to his angels. She kept insisting until he said yes, feeling it was cruel to continue to refuse a woman in her circumstances. Even after he agreed to come, he argued with himself. Let the angels wait for one night. What was the big deal? Let them wait.

The late Mrs. Rice's house was a grand old bosomy matron draped in stone swags and ornamented with carvings of flowers that might once have grown in the garden. Such an upright Victorian, it had, perhaps by moral force, withstood the bad days the neighborhood had endured with all its original stained and leaded glass windows intact. Even hoodlums, generations of hoodlums, the Irish, the Italians, the young black fellows in sheepskin coats, had had respect. Leopoldine led him past the foyer into the place he'd never seen.

"Poor Mrs. Rice," he said. Her nieces and nephews had picked the carcass of her longtime home to the bones with shameful abandon. One cat-clawed armchair sat in the parlor, too raggedy to be of value to the pickers. Where the other furniture ought to have been he saw coaster marks and a shaped change in the shade of the floorboards. The tiered glass chandelier teetered on frayed cord, ready to drop. The shoe man backed away from it.

"They couldn't get it down," said Leopoldine.

"Vultures."

Leopoldine shrugged her shoulders. She tapped an oak file that had been jimmied open. Newspaper articles saved for some forgotten reason, papers, bills and files were scattered across the inlaid floor. "They came looking for her fortune."

"Cash?"

"They were looking for cash." Leopoldine smiled. "And they got furniture."

"Serves them right," said the shoe man.

"But it was very good furniture." The kitchen cabinets were open. Only the cracked or incidental pieces remained on the shelves. The sink was full of Coca-Cola cans left by the thirsty scavengers. The sour stench embarrassed Leopoldine. "They unplugged the refrigerator. Electric cost money."

"But what about you?"

Leopoldine shrugged again. "I'm s'posed to be out already. How many years I'm with her? And they treat me like a thief. Ha!" The toaster was gone but the crumbs that had gathered under it remained. Leopoldine swept them into her hands. "They took the wastebasket." She shook the crumbs into the sink. "Need a coffee pot?" Leopoldine handed the shoe man a percolator.

"They didn't take this."

"Too old. Not old enough. It wants a shine, that's all. Perfectly good."

The shoe man followed her down the hall. The wainscoting was carved to resemble ivy tumbling over a trellis. "It's a beautiful house."

"You should have seen it. She had everything just so." She opened the etched glass door to Mrs. Rice's bedroom. On the floor lay piles of dresses. Mrs. Rice's white lingerie was dumped in a pile in the corner. Only her shoes, several pairs, black and tan on one rack, woven and white on another, remained in perfect order.

The shoe man opened a closet door. There hung the old blonde mink. "They left the mink."

"One of the kids wanted it for play but her mama said it probably had moths."

"I never saw her out of that coat."

"She loved it."

"It was part of her."

"What would you think if I took it?"

"You deserve to have it. At the very least."

"Yes," said Leopoldine. "I believe I do. I did love that old woman. Much as my own blood. And I tell you she would keel over an' die if she seen what they did . . ." Leopoldine waved her hand over the litter that was left of Mrs. Rice's life. "Keel right over an' die."

A dumped box of ivory face powder marked the place where the vanity had been. He kneeled to pick up a pink ostrich powder puff. He put it to his face. "Soft."

Leopoldine reached for it. She touched it to her cheek and gave it back. "Keep it," said Leopoldine.

He put the puff in his pocket as, still on his knees, he reached for a plain black accordion folder overturned on the floor. The shoe man righted it. It was filled with loose photographs, years' worth of memories. "They left these?"

"I told you. Her so-called family didn't give one damn about that dear old woman. I told you that."

The shoe man fingered the pictures. He had no such pictures of his own. Was old Mrs. Rice the pretty girl standing in front of a new car? There were several identical prints of a plain two-story beachfront hotel with white Adirondack chairs out front, empty chairs. What happened there and with whom? Who were the friends mugging in front of that rough waterfall? Three men and a boy with fishing rods and a gun. Did they grill their catch or come home empty? And who had the boy grown up to be? What happened in the house with flowers crowding the front door? Leopoldine had said Mrs. Rice was childless. A laughing mother and crying child sat on the front steps. Who were they? "Poor Mrs. Rice," he said. How he envied her.

"Take them," said Leopoldine.

Realizing the time, Leopoldine and the shoe man decided they were hungry. They walked to the Chinese for sweet and sour pork. Leopoldine wore the blonde mink as they ate. The shoe man noticed she was graceful with chopsticks and that she had a pretty face.

The waiter brought four orange slices and two fortune cookies. "You can have both," said Leopoldine.

The shoe man walked her back to the house. She kissed him on the cheek. The shoe man held his head very still, not daring to move it even slightly. He wondered if Leopoldine was waiting for him to take her in his arms.

He coughed to clear his throat. "Why didn't you marry?"

"I got a sister in the Bahamas," she said, as if that were enough of an answer.

Still feeling the wet where her lips had been, he pressed the accordion envelope under his arm and stepped into the dark. Avoiding shadows and doorways, he scurried along the curb from streetlight to streetlight, carefully scanning the sidewalks and passing cars for anyone who might stop him and take Mrs. Rice's photographs. Now they were his. He knew their worth. They were evidence of a life lived, proof that at least one person cared about one moment long enough to freeze it, proof there was a time other than now, a treasure of times, a treasure of times he might have had if the time he lost Angela had never come and gone. He gripped the handle of Mrs. Rice's coffee pot so that he could bash on-rushing hoodlums on the head. He was ready to defend the pictures, ready to fight, but nobody bothered him.

LUCILLE

E ven though the shoe man lingered at the red-topped table drinking coffee perked from Mrs. Rice's percolator, he arrived at the shop a half hour before his usual time. As he crossed Flatbush, he noticed a dark-windowed station wagon with the words *Black Pearl* painted on the side doors idling in the crosswalk in front of Reliable Repair. He knew the car was waiting for him. Waiting for him and he was early. Suddenly, he saw his own death, the car accelerating, himself being crushed. But that isn't what happened at all. Leopoldine lowered the back seat window and shouted, "Hey!" The shoe man dropped his keys. Leopoldine opened the door, setting one foot on the curb. She was wearing the black pumps he'd given her.

He traded one unreasonable fear for another and approached the taxi. Leopoldine wore Mrs. Rice's blonde mink coat buttoned up to her neck. The buttonholes strained across her chest. Her face was damp from perspiration. Leopoldine beckoned him closer. "What if I said there was a miracle?"

"It happens."

She put her mouth so close to his ear that her breath tickled. He was afraid she would declare her love, but she didn't, and he was almost disappointed. "What if I said that this here old coat had I don't know how many hundred-dollar bills, cash money, sewn ten deep right between the lining and the fur?" she whispered.

"Then I would say there was justice in this world," the shoe man answered.

She almost asked him to run with her, almost. He almost wished she had. But she didn't. Couldn't. And he put the thought out of mind. She meant to make him write his name and address, but she forgot. He meant to ask her where she was going, but the words never came from his mouth. Hoping that Leopoldine was on her way to the airport, that she would fly home to the sunny island of her birth and bask in her miracle, glory in her accidental wealth, he watched the Black Pearl roll into Flatbush traffic. Then he unlocked the shop and sat down to eat two pecan sticky buns at the bench in the window.

He was licking the sweet off his fingers when Lucille came into the shop. He didn't know she was Lucille at the time. He had never seen her walking past his window, which didn't mean she hadn't. He didn't know who she was. In that sense he wasn't far behind poor Lucille herself, who on that day knew who she wasn't and who she didn't want to be and that she needed her good shoes repaired if she was going to find work. She placed a pair of nicked navy blue calfskin dress pumps on his bench and asked if he thought they could be made like new. The leather-covered wood heels were battered as if she'd slid up and down between the metal bars of a sidewalk vent. The insole was worn through on the left shoe and the right shank needed support. This was more than a technical diagnosis. Without having yet looked closely at her face, the shoe man determined that his new customer didn't have money to spare, she was unwise, a little reckless, maybe easily distracted, not especially vain, and if she was in love, she was not loved in return. He rarely misinterpreted a customer's shoes, but he was a man like other men. He looked up from her shoes and saw wanting in her face. What did she want? The wanting gave a searing poignance to her features. Another girl with the same nose eyes mouth but without the wanting would have been unnoticeable, plain. This girl was somehow a beauty, a beauty with plain brown hair, plain not-quite-any-colored eyes, chapped lips and colorless skin.

She looked at him as if what he was about to say to her about her navy calfskin shoes was one of the most important things she would ever hear. He spoke carefully. "It can be done. Whether it should be done, I don't know."

She rubbed her forefinger across her rough lips. "Um, how much do you think it would cost? To make them nice, I mean."

"Six-fifty." He could not help but undercharge her. "Address?"

She didn't understand.

He tapped the sole of her right shoe. "It's my system."

"Ah!" She smiled and he felt handsome and young. "I'm staying with a friend. Six-ninety Carson Street, apartment seven." The shoe man wrote 690C. "Do you need a deposit? I could leave three. I need the rest 'til I get to the bank."

"No, I know you'll be back."

"What's your name?" she asked as if it were the most natural question.

The shoe man was used to seeing his name on junk mail, the rent bill, the phone bill, the gas and electric. He hadn't heard it out loud applied to himself since he didn't know when. "Just Jack." It sounded funny in his ears, as if he'd made it up on the spot. "Jack."

"Hi, Jack," she said easily. "I'm Lucille."

When he returned home that evening, the sky was divided in four uneven bands. He admired the combination of colors.

Cobalt, marine grey, orange, burgundy. Not the usual, no. It was beginning to be clear to the shoe man that somehow the order in the world had shifted.

Not long before, he'd read in the *Post* that the official timekeepers, whoever and wherever they were, had added an extra second at the beginning of the year so that time could keep apace with the globe's rotations. Was that the cause? Could a second move the settled order aside? What if Angela had turned her ankle and missed her train that Sunday morning, would he be living in a Fort Lauderdale condominium watching his grandchildren play in the pool?

There was a do-it-yourself moving van outside the house next to his building. Several sweaty young men were shoving the last of Mrs. Rice's possessions up a teetering ramp. A woman in pearls was screeching, "Careful! Careful!" at the workers who were battering and stacking Mrs. Rice's furniture. Two men chattering in Hebrew latched the back doors and the van drove off, turning right on Vanderpole Avenue. The shoe man sat on his stoop and watched. As soon as it was gone, a second, smaller, van arrived. The shoe man regarded the unloading furniture with a pang. Mrs. Rice was gone and so was Leopoldine.

From his back room window the shoe man saw his new neighbor survey Mrs. Rice's earliest rosebuds. With a shear, he savaged the bushes, clipping an armload of long, budded stems and tossing them carelessly into a ceramic vase. That was only the start. Next, he marked his arrival by hammering a nail through the bark of Mrs. Rice's shady oak, which had grown unmarred to the height of several stories over at least a century's time, and hanging a white plaster dog head on the trunk. What a pissing dog, thought the shoe man. He wanted to shout at him to stop his offenses, but he didn't. Years in the city, years reading the *Post,* had taught him that no sane man chastised a stranger unless he was prepared to die on the spot. The shoe man wasn't prepared to die for the oak tree or the memory of Mrs. Rice. Regarding the change as more than a shame, he retreated to his kitchen.

Waiting for dark, the shoe man dined on a can of oil-packed Bumble Bee, tasting the tin as much as the fish. He didn't really notice. He didn't want to think about his awful new neighbor so he thought about the photographs propped side by side where wall met the red-topped table. He wondered if Leopoldine and the mink had reached their destination. He wondered whether things might have been different if he'd been bolder, and decided to be bolder he'd have to be a different man. And he puzzled over the wanting in Lucille's young face. Lucille. She had to be nineteen, twenty at most. Angela's age. Angela's age and at the same time old enough or young enough to be his granddaughter.

When the moon had risen, the shoe man returned to the back room to work. The oak had assumed her lacy nighttime silhouette. The plaster dog head didn't show. Surrounded by his own glittering host of angels, the shoe man forgot about the monstrous man next door as he burnished the gold-leaf boots of Raphael, angel prince of the sun. It was not his first Raphael. His beatific first held the yellowing curtains back from the window closest to the neighbor's yard. When Angela chose those curtains, they had had a daisy pattern. No more. The red in Raphael's cheeks had faded in the spot where the light hit his face every fair-weather day. The new Raphael would guard the gated window by the fire escape. The neighborhood had suffered more crime of all kinds in the last twelve months than in the two years past combined. This time, the shoe man had carved an enraged Raphael. Under this angel's brow, his dense onyx eyes blackened the light that touched them. His sharp-chinned profile, if seen from below, would warn away hoodlum intruders.

He had been a whole season at this Raphael, yet what seemed to be an undeterminable want of his own distracted the shoe man from the ecstatic fatigue he loved to feel as he worked to the finish of a well-carved angel. When the last of the gold leaf was as it should be, the shoe man looked away from his work and noticed that it was well past midnight. He decided to let the golden boots set, and with a glance back at his fierce angel, he locked the back room door behind him. The shoe man had come to expect that the finish of one angel meant a visit from the next one asking to be rendered. As he

31

lay in his nightly position, on his back in his bed with his head sunk between two pillows, he sensed a womanly presence.

The shoe man didn't know what to make of it. From what he knew of angels, which was more than most men, femininity was not to be found in the heavenly community. At least not often and never simply. There was Lilith. She was a handful. Married Adam. Boring sex life. Left him for Satan where things were a little bit hotter. And there was the ancient Pistis Sophia. She wasn't the beatific type. She wanted answers. Not little answers to little questions. Whoppers. Like what, if *what* was the word, was light. Mother of all, lover to her sons, she wasn't the kind of angel you found on your Christmas tree, and all in all, she gave God a run for his money. Sex sex sex. Where there was sex, tempted angels fell, demons were begotten. It was no wonder, then, that God kept women out of the firmament. He had read that angels had no sex at all, but it seemed to him that they, or at least the ones he had seen in pictures and in his mind at times like this, leaned more toward the male. It occurred to the shoe man that his own disposition toward carving them that way hinged on practicality. He had no model other than himself. When one of his angels required an earthly form, it was easiest to carve a body like his own. Now that he considered his own form unworthy, he used his earlier angels as visual lasts for the later. And as for wings,

Angie had been of great assistance. Sometimes he wondered if the great sculptors would have sneered at his methods, but he felt no shame about his own technique. It was his. And the angels were for his eyes alone. His eyes and the eyes of birds who flew past. Fine with him. He left crumbs on the sill for his singing audience in the half hope there would some-day be another bird like Angie. So now. Maybe a woman angel would fly onto the sill. He smiled at his own joke. A woman angel. A contradiction. If God wasn't having any, neither was he.

The presence didn't leave just because she'd been dis-missed. She stayed close beside him, even in his sleep, and the shoe man woke with the start or the remains of an erection, wishing he remembered his dreams. As the coffee perked, he hung the glowering Raphael and stood back to gather the effect. The fierce new Raphael made his other one seem even gentler in demeanor. They balanced nicely, and the shoe man considered the space between the two win-dows. Gabriel's one hundred forty wings spanned the width, but there was wall beneath the hem of Gabriel's gown. Not that he would, but if, just if, he were ever to carve a woman, she would go with Gabriel because Gabriel was the one who spoke to souls in the womb. Told them what they were in for as they made the steep descent from paradise to earth with a whole life to live before they could go home, *if* they could go home. No guarantees.

Again, the shoe man saw his new neighbor chopping at Mrs. Rice's garden. He was wearing a T-shirt and white undershorts soiled black on the seat. It was hard to imagine his neighbor had ever been a soul torn from paradise. Where the rose-covered trellis used to stand, the new neighbor seemed to be building a low fence of pine posts. And there hung the white plaster dog head. The new neighbor turned his face toward the sun. He looks like a fish. He looks like a bass whose mouth has been ripped by a hook, thought the shoe man.

That afternoon he had pizza at Gloria's. He was eager to share the horrible news of the new neighbor. There was nothing about her neighborhood that Gloria didn't want to know, though there were many things, like the angels, she could never have guessed.

"I have a new neighbor," he said.

"He was in here last night," answered Gloria. "Ate half a pie. Left the crust." Gloria was proud of her crust. It was crisp on the outside. The inside was soft like fresh bread.

"He looks like a bass with his mouth ripped on the side. Real angry. Like he was hooked and let loose to bleed," said the shoe man.

Gloria shook her head. "He looks like a mass murderer to me."

"Yeah," said the shoe man. "And he acts like one, too.

First thing he did was nail up a white plaster dog head. On Mrs. Rice's beautiful old oak. Poor Mrs. Rice would roll over . . ."

"I don't believe it."

The shoe man gave a bitter snort. "Alls I got to say is what an improvement. Mother nature could take some pointers. She's saying to herself right this minute she's saying, Why didn't I think of that? How come I didn't make all my trees with white plaster dog heads growing out the side?"

Gloria laughed. The two Albanians behind the counter laughed. "What are you laughing at?" Gloria said. Gloria didn't trust foreigners to get the joke and she didn't like anybody laughing at America. "By the way, I haven't seen Leopoldine."

The shoe man had nothing to say about that.

He was glad he returned to his bench when he did because pretty Lucille walked by and she waved at him. She waved and she winked. And he winked back.

He worked late at the shop that night. He was used to being at odds during the time between a finished angel and the start of one new, but if he knew who he was going to carve, he might have gone to the lumberyard or the library. Since the closest he had to an idea was one halfhearted erection, there was little he could do. The next angel would come when it came. He kept busy. The problem with keeping busy was that he used up the work there was to do in less time than it usually took to do it. And then he was left with even more time to fill.

Happily, spring was quickly tightening its grasp on the days. Winter dripped off the branches of the oak. The temperature rose fifteen degrees in one day and it stayed there. Puddles in the street dried before noon. The sun brightened. He sat with his angels and drank morning coffee, watching the mass murderer replace Mrs. Rice's azaleas with wood chips. The mass murderer wore a purple and blue striped cotton dress. He didn't like this fish-faced dress-wearing fellow at all, but it wasn't because of his looks or his clothes. The shoe man had lived in the city too long to be bothered by things like that. Though he told himself he ought to have suspected it from the start, the shoe man was shocked to find that the mass murderer had not been content with an ornamental plaster dog's head. In the ten days since he'd moved next door, the mass murderer had nailed six rusty Swiss cowbells directly beneath the dog's head. He had hauled a painted ceramic elephant into the yard and placed a garishly molded white metal bench beside it. He had nailed antlers to his back fence. He had buried St. Francis up to his feet next to the almost budding crocuses. He had rigged a giant chalet-style plastic bird feeder on a rope slung over the old oak's lowest branch and fixed a Nefertiti head on the fence across from the antlers. Worse, he had nailed a stamped tin trumpeting angel beside the Nefertiti, and worse still, he had placed a granite statue of the two-faced Aztec god Quetzalcoatl smack-dab, so that the side of life faced away from the shoe man's view and the savage death's head faced his window and all his angels.

The shoe man thought about buying a rifle and shooting it out of his sight.

That afternoon at lunch, he said as much to Gloria. Vic, an ex-vet ex-cop ex-security guard on disability, fed slices to each of his three docile pit bulls. "Nah," he said. "They don't even shoot deer with a rifle."

"When was the last time you shot a deer?" teased Gloria.

Vic ignored her. They were lovers, now and then. "These days you use an AK-47."

"Or an Uzi," said one of the Albanians.

"What do you know about Uzis?" said Gloria.

"You want find? Across strit." Across the street was a former bodega in which several Yemenites sold newspapers, out-of-date magazines and milk twenty-four hours a day and managed to pay the rent.

"Not you want find, *do* you want *to* find *out*." Through her blouse, Gloria gripped the sides of her brassiere and tugged it to a more comfortable position. Vic watched her make her adjustments. "Anyhoo, who gives a shit?" The shoe man paid for his slice and a take-out coffee and returned to the shop.

Anytime after lunch, sometimes as early as one, some-times as late as six, Lucille could be counted upon to walk past and wave and wink. What she carried varied, but she always had a hand free for him. Her pumps had been ready since the day after she left them. Better than new, he'd made them, reinforcing the construction so they'd last a marathon run, re-covering the heels with a nearly impossibly perfect match of navy leather he'd happened to have in the back. She would marvel at his work, he knew she would, but the shoe man was content to leave her shoes on the shelf. He was afraid that when she claimed them, it would mean an end to the winks and waves that made the minutes of his after-noons at the shop first succulent with suspense, then light with satisfaction at the sight of her. Without knowing how it had happened, exactly, he found himself delightfully swirling in a small side eddy. For the first time in years, he was a part of the onrushing spring. He winked once in prac-tice. She made him feel handsome. Let her shoes stay on the shelf, he thought to himself as he watched out the window of Reliable Repair while his hands did their usual work without his mind's supervision.

At three-thirty by the Kiwi polish wall clock, the shoe man saw Lucille scamper up the subway stairs. She was still a little breathless when she entered the shop. The bells tin-kled. "Jack!" she panted. "What a gorgeous day. And you're getting a tan right here in the window while I've been cooped up!"

The shoe man didn't know quite what to say. Here she was, and he wanted to keep her standing before him, maybe forever, exhaling his name. "By the end of the summer I'm brown as an Indian."

"You lucky duck! Either I'm white or I burn."

Jack knew just where her shoes were, 690C, but he inspected every cubbyhole as if he'd misplaced them.

"Six-ninety Carson," Lucille said helpfully. "But I'm not there anymore."

"Oh?"

"It didn't work out."

What didn't work out? Work out how? "Here they are, Lucille."

"You remember my name."

"Of course I remember your name," he said. "Lucille." He handed her the navy pumps. As she appraised them, he savored her delight.

She inspected the soles, the insoles, the uppers, the shanks, the stitching, the heels. "Oh, Jack, you're amazing. Incredible, really. These are beautiful, just beautiful." She bent at the waist to untie her sneakers. She tore off her gym socks and slid her red-painted toes into the pumps. The shoe man shyly permitted himself a look at her bare legs, muscu-

39

lar but not thick, unmarred, finer than the creamiest hide from a milk-fed calf, as if they'd never been bruised or scratched.

"The arch ought to be better now."

Lucille walked into the back shadows of the shop and out again, testing the fit. "They're heaven. I wish I had a lot of friends so I could send them all to you." She threw her sneakers in a canvas bag, paid him six-fifty exact and left the shop with a wave, no wink. "See you!" she said. He couldn't bear to watch her walk away.

True to his fears, the shoe man did not see Lucille the next day or the next day or the next. A week passed. For all he knew she was gone forever and he mourned the loss of her even as he scolded himself for his foolish old heart. He'd lost a wife. Who was Lucille?

One morning, all of the crocuses opened at once. Purple and yellow buds lined his walk to the shop. They bloomed at the bases of fire hydrants and mailboxes. They bloomed in gardens. They bloomed in driveways under the wheels of parked cars. He walked slowly, noticing the flowers out of duty to the better part of himself but not rejoicing in their beauty as he might have done on another day. He stopped at the Yemenites' for a *Post*. The Haitians were out of sticky buns, so he bought two ugly chocolate croissants. The commuters descended under the street to the train. The shoe man opened the shop and he opened the paper, but he didn't read even page one because that morning the shoe man understood his sadness. At least he thought he did. His Angela. His angel. The angel he'd been meant to carve. Lucille was all of these. She called him Jack. She had been sent to him. Now he was sure of it. Now she was gone.

WHAT THE SHOE MAN
DIDN'T KNOW

She wasn't gone. At least not gone the way the shoe man meant. In her own opinion, Lucille Bixby was as far from heaven as a girl could possibly be. She was at her mother's.

As usual, her mother was angry. She had sent Lucille's father to the store for a half gallon of milk and a Pennsylvania lottery ticket. Her request had been very specific. He was to play 1, 2, 9, 25, 6 and 62. The ticket in her hand read 4, 8, 66, 2, 7, 11. "Thanks for nothing," she said as she opened the milk carton. Lucille's father didn't answer. He was not in the practice of answering his wife. Lucille's mother put a better face on the matter than she would normally have done because not only was Lucille home for a visit, her sister, Lucille's aunt, had come east from Fordyce and she was busy baking blueberry muffins from scratch. She worked in sour silence and within the hour her kitchen was filled with the glorious aroma of a dozen sweet, hot muffins and fresh coffee. Lucille, her aunt and even her father hurried to the breakfast table.

"What a treat!" said Lucille's father, hoping to make some kind of amends.

Lucille held the basket of muffins under her nose and inhaled. "I could get drunk on this smell."

Lucille's mother smiled as she put the butter on the table. Lucille took a muffin and passed the basket. She sliced it open. It was perfection.

Lucille's aunt sliced hers, finding only two berries. "Oh, nuts! I like them loaded with blueberries."

"It must have been the last one from the bottom of the bowl," said Lucille. "Take another."

Lucille's mother opened her muffin. "I have too many." She looked at her sister's muffin. "I like it your way."

"Well, I like it your way."

"No, it's too fruity."

"I like it fruity," said Lucille's aunt.

"You miss the cake," said Lucille's mother.

"But the berries are the point," Lucille's aunt rejoined. Lucille's mother answered that they weren't and so on and on until Lucille could bear the discussion no longer.

She said, "Why don't you switch? You'll both have what you want."

Lucille's mother sighed heavily. "No," she said. Lifting her overly fruited muffin to her mouth, she took a bite. She chewed and swallowed. "This is the muffin I chose and this is the muffin I have to eat." She took another bite as she glared at her sister. "And the same goes for her."

That was that. Lucille decided that no matter how hard it was to survive in the city, it would be hell and insane to stay home one more day.

She waited in the drugstore next to the bus station. She perused the paperback rack, but reading on the bus made her sick. She wandered to the postcard rack. She had no use for cards saying *Scenic Pennsylvania*. Once she got on the bus, she was never coming back. And for the umpteenth time, she made up her mind about something else. Only this time she meant it. She was going to be famous.

She reached for a postcard of Marilyn Monroe. Now, that was famous. On damn near every forty-five-cent postcard rack in damn near every drugstore Lucille had ever been in, there she was, Marilyn Monroe, her eyes half shut, her lips wide open, twisting this way and that. In black and white and in color. Everyone wanted her. Wanted her picture to send to a friend or to stick on the fridge with a magnet. She got to sleep with presidents and geniuses and baseball stars and everybody loved her just for being alive. And Marilyn had been dead since God knew how long before Lucille was even born. Even already famous people wanted to be her instead of themselves. By Lucille's calculations, that was as famous as any girl could be. Her home economics teacher had mentioned the resemblance. So had her first boyfriend who had a car. So why not cash in on the one special thing she might possibly have and be famous instead of no one and nothing and stuck? So famous that They, whoever They were, would say her name the way They said Marilyn Monroe.

Famous people didn't have to eat the muffins they first chose. They could change their minds. They could have the whole basket all to themselves, with fourteen fresh berries in every single muffin if fourteen berries was what they wanted.

She was never going to be like her mother. She wasn't even going to be her simple self. Starting that very second, which was as good as any second when it came to starting, Lucille was going to be someone else.

Entirely.

She paid for the postcard and boarded the bus. She was going to be Marilyn. That was that.

The shoe man had had no reason to take Mrs. Rice's photographs off the red-topped table. He liked them there. But they pleased him less than he thought they would.

There were questions.

He read the photographs at least once a day in much the same comfortable way that he had, until he'd discovered sticky buns, read and reread breakfast cereal boxes as he ate his flakes. He didn't remember anything any of the backs of cereal boxes actually said. It was different with the photographs. They had come to be so familiar to his eyes that the women, men and children they depicted no longer seemed like strangers. It was almost as though he remembered them from some other time, but not quite.

There were no names written on the backs of the pictures. Over the years Mrs. Rice had obviously trusted to memory. In her old age, Mrs. Rice couldn't tell a dead parrot from a live one. Who knew what, in the end, she remembered? Her mother and father? Past husbands? Girlfriends from grammar school? Shipboard bridge partners met on a cruise? Would Mrs. Rice have remembered their names or the ship's destination or which husband shared her berth on that trip? Who knew? The shoe man wondered whether Mrs. Rice could have named names and places any better than he, who had never really known them. He wondered if, when Mrs. Rice had taken the photographs from the black envelope, *if* she had taken the photographs from the black envelope at all, she could picture the faces of people she once cared to remember with different expressions than the ones that were shown. Could she remember them as he remembered her? Before she died, did she see them as they were, long-legged or stumpy, running to catch a train, scraping mud off a shoe, sitting sated at the end of a meal, examining themselves in the bathroom mirror? As many times as he fingered the photographs, as familiar as the smiles became, the shoe man could never imagine past the moment shown inside the white borders. The people in the photographs had no life for him. They were grey-shaded scraps even though they had once actually lived, might still be alive, might live in the neighborhood. As much as he wanted to think that they could somehow substitute for memories he yearned for and lacked, they weren't as real as his lost Angela, his angels, his Angie, Lucille. They weren't even as real as the dreams he forgot, which were his, after all, and which was a shame, he thought, on yet another morning when young leaves and blooms seemed to open toward the early sun in front of his very eyes.

On his way to work, the shoe man passed the mass murderer. They did not acknowledge each other. Before he turned his head away, the shoe man noticed that his bass-mouthed neighbor had an inch-wide hole in the right toe of his scuffed moccasin through which the shoe man could see his scaly greyish toenail. He remembered reading that mankind had originally come from the sea. Here's one of the ones they ought to throw back, he thought. The shoe man considered it unlikely the mass murderer would ever seek the services of Reliable Repair. That was just as well. He might be tempted to leave one tack exposed, to give this man just one little prick in memory of Mrs. Rice's garden.

He lunched at Gloria's. Gloria remarked, in the same words she'd used every day for the past several days, that he hadn't been himself.

He knew she was right and that he wouldn't be himself

until his mind was busy with a block of wood, a block of wood that would become an angel under his knife. And that wouldn't happen until he had an angel's face, body, wings and spirit clear in his mind.

"So who have I been?" he asked testily. Lucille, his missed chance, seemed to block the visit of another vision. He thought about carving a quick Lucille from memory just so that he could get rid of her and move on to whichever angel was now hiding from him, but Lucille had left a feeling more than a face. There was nothing to do but wait for the feeling to fade. It would fade. He knew that. What a shame, he thought to himself as he licked tomato sauce from his fingers, what a shame for that bittersweet twinge to go dull and what a nuisance if it didn't. It wasn't doing him any damn good, that was sure.

It was the type of an afternoon when people in the neighborhood found excuses to walk out of doors by running their practical errands. Because taking shoes for repair in the spring is high on the list of what needs to be done, Reliable Repair was filled with customers mingling duty with pleasure. One by one, they remarked to the shoe man that it was the most splendid day. He agreed with the comment so many times that at some point he forgot he was glum and began to believe that the day was indeed quite extraordinary.

Extraordinary or not, his heart tightened when, as he

glanced out the window at four forty-five, a red-mouthed woman unknown to him, a blonde in tight capri pants, passed his window, winked right at him and waved in the same way Lucille used to do.

What have I done so wrong, he wondered as he yet again agreed out loud that it was a splendid day.

The customer whose loafer he held seemed not to have noticed either the winking blonde or the shoe man's sudden distress. "And can you uncurl the tassels so they lie flat?" asked the customer.

"No problem," said the shoe man, writing the customer's address on the sole.

As the sun hid behind the tower of the Williamsburg bank, the silvery hour marks on the giant clock extended past their limits to join with the points of a radiant halo. It was too much to hope for. It might have been the sun, the shoe man thought to himself, and the dusty glare. The windows need washing. Her hair was white-yellow. "The sun in my eyes," he said, but saying it didn't make it so. When the sun had disappeared from the borough of Brooklyn but was still somewhere close enough to keep full darkness from the sky, the shoe man locked his shop and hurried home, only stopping to buy a quart of chocolate ice cream and a beer from the Korean grocers. Gloria had told him Koreans didn't care for the easy American smile, considered it phony, but the cashier smiled at him and said, "Have nice night," as the shoe man counted his change. It was correct. The sun was not adequate explanation for the blonde. He had seen her as clearly as he saw the coins in the palm of his hand. Furthermore, there was the matter of what she did. She winked. She waved. At him.

What did it mean?

He knew he wasn't young, but he had not considered his mind untrustworthy. She might be the first little lapse. He might go from blondes to flying terriers. He might stare at a shoe unable to remember what the customer wanted done, or worse, he might forget his craft. He might leave the stove burning after his morning coffee was poured and come home to his angels in ashes. And maybe one day he might not know his angels, might not know his own home. Damn Angela! How could she leave him alone to grow old? He could barely see the keyhole in his door for the tears he was crying.

Leaving his ice cream on the table, he unlocked the back room and turned on the light. His angels surrounded him. "Why should you torment me?" he shouted. The angels kept their wooden silence. He let himself slowly be calmed by their beauty. They were beautiful from the loving work of his hands; the love he might have wasted had gone to them. He sat amongst them late into the night, letting the cool chocolate slip soothingly down his throat. Things were not as bad as they had seemed. So his mind had made a little slip or the sun had played a trick. Big deal. It had never happened before. It might never happen again. He took the beer to bed and slept soundly.

The business brought in by the fair weather made it easy for him to avoid looking out at the street and keep his eyes to his cobbler's bench. That was what he decided to do. He did not want to risk another frightening little trick.

At lunch, a big fellow whose pants hung low to expose his moon-white buttocks carried a box that held a portable television into the pizzeria. He offered it for sale. Gloria was about to chase him out when, to everyone's surprise, the shoe man said, "How much?"

Gloria sneered. "First you want a gun, now this."

"It's brand new. Never used," said the fellow.

"Don't give me that crap," said Vic protectively. "Plug her in."

The fellow put the box up on Gloria's counter and pulled the small set out of its hard foam cushion. "Still has the guarantee."

"No guarantee if it fell off a truck. Cut the bull and plug her in." The picture was crisp, the vividness of the transmitted reds, greens, violets and flesh tones made their real-life counterparts look dead by comparison. "You want her?" Vic asked the shoe man.

The shoe man had had a television for about a decade a

decade or two ago. He watched Huntley and Brinkley until one or the other or both retired. After that, news wasn't the same and when his set began to broadcast shadow and static, he put it on the curb outside his building for anyone to take. He hadn't missed television, but he thought it might be of use to him now, might sit nicely at the red-topped table and talk to him, might protect him somehow. "For a price."

"Two hundred," said the white-bottomed fellow.

"He'll give you twenty-five."

"Shit, man . . ."

"You're lucky I don't bust you right here and now," said Vic, flashing out-of-date police ID. The deal was done. The shoe man bought Coca-Colas all round to celebrate before he returned to work.

That evening he moved Mrs. Rice's photographs to make room for the set on the table. He pressed the "on" switch and immediate chatter crowded his kitchen. It was too much and he pressed it "off." Enough for one night. He pressed the button again. On. Off. It changed even the silence. He thought his purchase was probably good, but too sudden a change. He'd have to get used to it. Slowly.

The next morning, the sun skulked behind a pillar of black clouds. By afternoon he was sorry he hadn't watched the weather forecast and he was sorry he hadn't carried his umbrella. He had umbrellas in the shop, but if he opened

53

one, he couldn't sell it, so the shoe man decided lunch would wait until the rain let up. He had plenty to do. He wasn't that hungry.

The bell on his door jingled unexpectedly and then she walked in, his red-mouthed sun-trick blonde, his apparition, dripping wet and sniffling. She might have been the death's head side of Quetzalcoatl for the look of fear on his face.

"You okay?" said the vision.

"Where did you come from?" he whispered. What did it mean? She couldn't be dust. She wasn't glare. She was standing before him. He wanted to test. To pass his hand through her body and prove her an illusion. If she was an illusion, what did it mean? Had he left the coffee burning on the stove? Was this his angel? Was he going to die?

The vision wiped her wrist across her nose. "The Y. I was halfway here and all of a sudden it was cats and dogs. I needed you to fix something for me."

The shoe man examined her dense brown eyes for a clue. As she moved closer, he decided she was certainly real, if real was flesh and the smell of water-soaked wool. She was even familiar.

She giggled. "My belt. It needs an extra hole." She held a length of red leather out to him. "Here."

The shoe man punched a hole where she wanted a hole and cautiously handed back the belt.

"Thanks, Jack," she said. "You're a doll."

"Who are you?"

"I'm Lucille," said Lucille, tapping the corner of her right eye with a fingernail that matched her lips. "Contacts." She popped one out onto the tip of her finger and there she stood, one no-particular-color eye, one brown. "See? It's my Marilyn look. See?" She fanned the wet strands of her hair. "Champagne Blonde."

"No," he protested, though he believed her.

"Bottle magic. You like?"

The shoe man didn't know how to answer. "It's a miracle." The shoe man did not know how to feel. How could he know? The burden of a miracle. What did it mean? What was he to do about it? "I'm too old for this," he mumbled.

"Don't be silly." Lucille giggled again. Within the month she would be sleeping in his double bed.

on't assume too much. Putting two and two together doesn't always equal four, and just because the spicier papers and the local TV flat-out said that theirs was a most unsavory union, used words like *wicked, sex starved* and that all-time favorite *grasping arms,* doesn't make it so, now does it? Grasping sex-starved wicked arms sell papers and papers sell ads and ads sell products and God bless America, as Gloria would say.

So. Upon her return from her mother's, Lucille booked herself a bleak room at the Newsome Street Y and did something about her nothing hair. She took her color postcard of Marilyn Monroe in 1954 to Duane Reade. Half an aisle was devoted to hair color. Most of the shades available were blonde. Lucille patiently compared the photo on each box with the photo she held in her hand. Easy Care Champagne Blonde came the closest. She paid out six bucks for the kit.

Becoming Champagne Blonde was a six-hour smelly process. First she stripped all the brown from her hair. Then she colored the mass of damp translucent shafts. The dye stung her eyes until she wept. When her hair was dry, she stared at herself in shock. Oh, her hair was very, very Marilyn, but her no-particular-color eyes seemed suddenly smaller, her face newly sallow. Misery.

There was nothing to do but go to bed and hope she would dream a solution.

She did. In the morning she returned to the pharmacy. Red lipstick, white shadow, black liner and a powdery parchment base. Marilyn makeup. It made all the difference.

Feeling lucky at last, Lucille circled several ads in the paper. The first job she applied for, she got.

She began work at a cocktail bar owned by two snide Europeans. The tips were good though she was in no way a natural waitress. One of the girls showed her how to wet her tray before so that bills would stick when the customer went to pick up his change. Customers were free to peel the money off the tray, but she would smile her new Marilyn smile and they would almost always leave the extra. At the end of her first two weeks' work, she paid her bill at the Y and bought some new and tighter, more Marilyn clothes. It had become clear to her that even with the makeup, her own natural eyes marred the Marilyn look. She treated herself to a pair of brown-tinted nonprescription contact lenses at the Two-Hour Eyewear Shop. Simple problem. Simple solution. It pleased her to think Mother never would have thought of it.

As she altered her looks, Lucille felt protected, as if her new self shielded the old from itself. She couldn't say why being blonde and brown-eyed and Marilyn-lipped made her feel more confident. It just did. And not only was she getting the hang of being a blonde, she was being a blonde in the city of cities, on her way to being a blonde in the widest of worlds. A woman of the world, she would be. London, Paris and Rome. The right wines. All that stuff. And meanwhile, she held her pocketbook smartly at the latch. She stopped worrying that all black men were muggers. She positioned and pushed and shouldered for a seat on the subway train. She wore her waitress skirt short, to show her lean thighs. As she did her job, she smiled smiled smiled and she called her male customers handsome whether they were or not.

One especially busy afternoon, a party of eight truly handsome men sat in her section. They all ordered more than one drink. They all ordered filet mignon on French bread. After they ate and drank and laughed, they all ordered Irish coffee. Anticipating a heavenly tip, she took care to top the eight mugs with perfect whipped cream peaks and to dust the peaks with just the right amount of nutmeg. When she returned to the table, the eight men had gone without paying the check. Her boss had no sympathy. It was her fault, he said, and she would pay for the whole meal herself, melting whipped cream and all.

She was too busy to stop and cry. When the men at the nearest table asked what was wrong, she said, "Nothing," but she couldn't quite back up the lie with a smile. They asked her a second and third time, until she figured maybe they cared. She told them about the drinks and the filets and the way she'd been tricked into turning her back with a complicated order for eight Irish coffees.

"They were dogs."

"Ruddy mongrels."

"Swine."

"And it all comes straight out of my pocket," she said.

"We'll help you with that," said a man who spoke his words as if he pulled them on a rubber band. He pulled a pin from his lapel, a plastic kiwi bird that looked like real gold. "Cheer you up." She took the bird from his hand and pinned it to her apron. "It's a kiwi, like me," he said. "From New Zealand."

Lucille touched the bird. "Someday I'd like to go to New Zealand."

"Where men are men and sheep are nervous."

Lucille had heard that old joke more often than she'd

heard the "Star-Spangled Banner." She'd heard it applied to Australians, the English, to Texans and Hoosiers and men from Montana. Midwesterners substituted cattle for sheep, Middle Easterners substituted camels. Still she laughed. Their kindness and the hope of a helpful tip restored her mood. "Thank you."

"That's much better," said the New Zealander. "Isn't it, love?"

She bustled round her station, employing her Marilyn charm once again. The hostess seated another large group, and just after she passed out the menus, the New Zealander signaled to her for another round. She tapped her kiwi and turned toward the bar. On her way, her new customers stopped her to ask which of the listed specials were left. At the end of her brief recitation, she looked up from her order pad and saw an empty table where her new friends had been. She knew what they'd done. She'd told them how to do it. The boss dragged her across the room by the arm. He demanded her money. She handed it over, all of it. It wasn't enough.

Lucille was fired. She didn't argue. She would have fired herself. She felt smaller than the smallest small-town rube. She felt as if some invisible witness were cackling "fool" in her ear. Some Marilyn. Some woman of the world. Fool me once. How did it go? Fool me once, shame on you. Fool me twice, shame on me. She was not the kind of girl to take an oath never to trust anybody again. Never to trust was not in her nature. What she could do, she did. On the sidewalk, before she descended into the subway station, Lucille promised herself she would keep that gold plastic kiwi the rest of her life. And she would learn, she would triumph, if it killed her.

The shoe man didn't know about her promises. He saw her ascend the subway steps at an earlier hour than usual. She didn't look up at him. He tapped the glass. She didn't seem to hear. Leaving his bench, he opened the door. Seeing her smudged black-and-red-rimmed eyes, he said, "Lucille, what's wrong?"

"Oh, Jack," she answered, and began to cry. He led her to the same chair Leopoldine and so many other women had cried in.

She had no money. She'd spent every penny, expecting the money she'd had in her purse to cover the rent and the food and to keep coming in week after week. It was Friday. If she couldn't pay the Y, she couldn't stay there. The shoe man told her not to worry. Before he realized what he was saying, he'd offered her his own bed. "I have a couch." He shocked himself but he repeated the offer. "I'll sleep on the couch." To the shoe man's further astonishment, Lucille accepted. She said yes the way she said Jack, as if it were the

most natural thing. On that day, at that time, in Lucille's
opinion, it wasn't whether or not his kindness was the natural thing. It was the only thing.

That evening, the shoe man accompanied Lucille to the Newsome Street Y. He settled her bill while she gathered her things. The weight of her suitcase and her repeating promise to pay him back prevented the shoe man from thinking ahead. Excepting his cherished, uncritical Angie, he had never had a houseguest. Angela couldn't be called a houseguest. She was his wife. Except for the back room, filled with his pleasure, his tools and uncountable angels, the apartment he called his home was so familiar to him that he hadn't actually seen it in years. Now he wondered anxiously how it would look, how he would look, through Lucille's eyes. He was afraid of what she'd see.

Holes in his socks? Mildew? His habits? Dust bunnies? His angels?

The shoulder strap of Lucille's suitcase cut a furrow in his shoulder and he wanted to lie down on his bed and close his eyes for fifteen minutes so that he could consider the sudden turn his life had taken. It was too late for that.

Instead of walking directly home, he took Lucille to his usual take-out place for eat-in Chinese. Lucille rolled lo mein around her fork. She sucked the brown noodles in between her lips. A shiny trail of chili oil divided the fullness.

She looked like an ordinary, hungry girl, not like an angel, not at the moment, but the shoe man wasn't fooled. Entertaining angels unawares, he thought to himself as he dipped his breaded pork first in the duck sauce and then in the mustard the way he always did. It occurred to him that it might be *she* who was somehow unaware of who she was. Maybe she was occupied by an angel. Possessed. He hadn't heard of it, but if a devil could claim an unsuspecting man, why couldn't an angel claim Lucille? Her red lipstick marked the thick teacup. Angela used to leave her lip prints everywhere. There were just too many signs to ignore. She was a gift, his woman on the windowsill, his model. At last he could begin again. And if she was unaware, what did it matter? There was no reason to mention his plans or his secret room full of angels. Not yet. A female angel might flit away. She might take offense. She might be frightened. The time would come. He would know the right time and accept no other. Having made that decision, he relaxed and asked Lucille if she would join him in an order of pineapple cubes.

"You're a doll," she answered as he raised a hand to hail the waitress.

She didn't ask about the closed door off the kitchen. On the way home he'd practiced evasions in his head, what to say if she asked, but Lucille showed no curiosity about his angel room. Her lack of curiosity threw his thinking out of line. Maybe she already knew.

Lucille knew nothing. What the shoe man didn't know was that when she accepted his offer, she had accepted him. To her eyes, the shoe man's place looked just the way it should. After a day or two, she wondered about the closed door. More than once she tested it, found it locked and asked no questions, but that was different. On their first night together, there were no questions to be asked. Things were the way they were and she was grateful. The tops of hard objects were softened with dust fuzz. That was good. It gave her something she could do for him and she wanted to do something for this sweet little wiry-haired old man.

The bed, the armchair, the dresser, the mirror, the kitchen table and the knickknacks were the unelaborate furniture she'd seen on reruns of TV shows made before she was born.

Mom and Dad furniture. Not her Mom and Dad, but the happy Mom and the wise Dad and the kids who always learned their lesson. "Do you have kids?" she asked.

The shoe man pulled at his belt loops and said, "Let me get you some clean sheets. I got extra. Wait right here." She had stripped the bed by the time he returned with the linens. Together they spread the top sheet and the blanket, folding hospital corners. "Hasn't looked that good since 1952," said the shoe man.

"Woman's touch," said Lucille.

Angela's words. Another sign. "Who used to say that?" he tested.

Lucille fluffed one of the two pillows and tossed it into his arms. "My mom."

"You'll be wanting your beauty rest," said the shoe man. He promised himself he would take better than good care of her. Give her no reason to disappear. "Take any towel except the green one. The rest are clean."

The shoe man lay on the back room couch and listened to the water run as Lucille splashed her face. He heard the slight scratching of her toothbrush and the flush of the toilet. Hearing the extreme lightness of her step as she returned to his bedroom, he was sure of her angelic aspects. He heard the bed sigh slightly as her womanly body pressed the old mattress. How that bed used to wheeze when he and Angela tumbled, a plait of legs and arms, sweating and sighing and trying to make that baby out of him and her. Angela made him oil the spring coils so the neighbors couldn't eavesdrop on their passions. The shoe man never thought about what the neighbors thought anymore. Back then he hadn't cared but to please her, which was all he wanted to do. He bought a tiny red tin can with a stiff little spout. Slip-R-E Devil all purpose oil. Angela called him her slippery devil after that. And he called her angel face, which was why he had started with angels in the first place. For years he kept the can of Slip-R-E Devil oil on his night table to remind him and then, because it reminded him, he'd one day thrown it away.

The squishy pillows of the back room couch held a perfect memory of his shape. He was the only one who sat on that couch. All indentations were his. He'd napped there many an afternoon, but he had no hope of sleep that night, not with Lucille breathing slowly in his bed. Surrounded by the dark geography of his angels, on the ceiling, on the floors, on the windows, on the walls, curves and peaks, no details, he knew the place and the shape of each one in spite of night blindness. He had carved their expressions, not always knowing why he'd chosen what he did. Sometimes the knife had decided for him. A slip caused the pious purse of angelic lips to be refashioned into a grin now and then.

Were there hundreds of silent faces now? He thought about counting them, but he didn't want to know exactly how many angels lived in his room. The number was never the point and the count might take sleep farther from his reach. His angels were still. The only movement betrayed was that caused by the shadows of the wind-tussled oak leaves outside the window and his own restless shifting. He wished his angels would talk to him. He heard Lucille murmur in her sleep.

He waited for dawn, which came in shades of grey, as if the mud-covered sun were being dragged up out of a swamp. He watched the mass murderer weed his garden, listening as Lucille's washing sounds rose and fell to a silence when he might take his own shower.

"Morning, Jack!" she twittered as he undressed behind the door.

"Morning!" he shouted back, thinking how lucky he was after all to hear his name spoken by her first thing on a cloudy morning. Stepping into the shower, he breathed the perfume left by her shampoo. Not a single strand of her hair remained. He saw that she'd scrubbed the black mildew from the grout. The smooth porcelain was white surrounded by white, no rings, no smudges. With his green towel wrapped around his waist, he hesitated in the bathroom. "All clear?" he called.

"All clear!"

He scuttled barefoot into the bedroom for a change of socks and undershorts. The bed was neatly made. Lucille had tidied away all signs of her night there. The shoe man was disappointed at the missing traces and resolved to ask her straight out to fill the place with her self and her smell, to scatter her feminine things, to call him Jack.

She perked his coffee in Mrs. Rice's pot. She knew the way he liked it without having to ask. "I haven't slept so well since I don't know," she said.

The shoe man stirred a spoonful of sugar into his cup. "Me neither." He took a sip. "I don't know, uh, what your plans . . ."

"Oh, I'll find a job . . ."

"What your plans, but you're welcome to stay for as long as . . ."

"Until I find a job . . ."

"As long as you want." He blushed. "No rush. I like the company."

"I won't be in your way?"

"That's what I like. You're in my way."

Lucille's shiny red lips opened into a laugh. "You're a perfect honeypot! Now, what's for breakfast around this joint?"

The shoe man took her for sticky buns. She read the want ads as he set up his bench. The shoe man told her not to rush into a lousy job. She should find something that suited her, something right, not just any job, especially since the rent was covered. She accepted that too, and asked how she would ever be able to pay him back. He said she already had, but over the next few days the shoe man found that even living with an angel like Lucille required adjustments.

He had to close the bathroom door and mind the noises that he made. Sometimes Lucille stood in front of the sink rubbing white powder on the lids of her eyes, or painting black liner across them with her lips apart and her tongue out as if for balance just when he might have liked to shave or read the *Post* on the toilet seat. Sometimes Lucille, who was very tidy, put things away where he couldn't find them, and because she folded her towel in thirds he felt obliged to do the same. He bought four packs of white Fruit of the Loom T-shirts, a total of eight brand new V-necks, figuring seven days of the week plus one for laundry, so that he wouldn't be ashamed of the way he looked sitting in his own chairs. The price had gone up five times since the last time he had made such a purchase. Five times. And he'd had to buy new socks. A woman in the house was expensive in little ways. On the other hand, Lucille brought economies. She got the best price on paper napkins and detergent, buying family size instead of the small packages he was used to. And she liked to cook. She made muffins, blueberry muffins, strawberry muffins, banana-nut muffins with little black flecks, and sticky buns with brown sugar chunks and pecans on top that made him forget the Haitian sticky buns, at a savings of $2.30 a day.

Lucille liked to watch his TV. She liked it in the morning
with coffee. The first nights, after he'd closed himself in the
angel room and she'd supposedly gone to bed, he'd hear low
chuckling from the kitchen. Lucille liked the talk shows at
night. Now that Lucille lived with him, the shoe man didn't
like TV at all. It was a poor substitute for her company, and
now that Lucille lived with him, when he was not in her
company, he was rich with the pleasure of having finally
begun to work on his woman angel.

The weather was his ally. She wore her short shorts and
cropped tank tops unselfconsciously. Her proportions were
his to study. She sat stillest when she watched TV. Nonethe-
less, he could not learn to abide the distraction of impersonal
chatter drowning the sweet rhythm of her breathing. To
Lucille's delight, he moved the set off the kitchen table and
on to the top of the dresser in her bedroom. Her bedroom,
that was how he thought of it now, even though the bed was
his and half the drawers were filled with his things.

Lucille liked to talk. As her life had been short and dull by
her own description, most of her conversation was about a
future that seemed to the shoe man to be impassable miles
from where she sat and extraordinarily grand. Marilyn
Monroe, she said, admitting she'd never seen her movies,
only her photographs, eyes half shut, mouth wet and wide.
She did an imitation. The shoe man said it was good. When
Lucille was in the mood to talk about how her life would one

day be—the heated pool, the maids, the limos, the clothes and him, near her, but in his very own cottage on the grounds of her estate—he listened more to the sound of her voice than her words as he sketched her moods and movements, her hands and face, from all angles.

She never asked why he drew page after page of just her, though she did ask for one sketch. "You have more talent in your little finger . . ." she told him. "You'll do my official portrait and stuff if you want." He let himself laugh at that. She didn't take offense.

One evening as they sat at the red-topped table, she wondered out loud what Marilyn looked like in 3-D. "I mean, pictures, you know. You can't be sure. I heard once there was more than one. I mean, they used doubles and stuff."

"No," said the shoe man. "There was only one. I saw her once. Me and my wife saw her on a sidewalk out in front of Radio City." It was the first time he'd mentioned a wife.

"Jack!" Lucille shook his arm. "I can't believe you haven't said! What did you see? Tell me exactly. Every detail. You were standing where? And was she smiling or what? Did she see you? Did you see her face? Was she like with the president or anything?"

"It was hard to see much. There were people around. I saw fur and a hat, mostly. White fur."

"That was all?"

The shoe man was sorry to disappoint her. He tried to remember more. "Well . . ."

"Men are terrible at details."

Not wanting to be like other men, Jack slid his pencil into the sketchbook's spiral binding and drew an hourglass in the air with his hands. "She had it all in the right places."

"Oh, Jack."

"She wasn't a skinnybones."

"Like me," she said.

"You're just right the way you are." Since the day she'd first come to stay in his bed, the shoe man pretended to himself and to her that her body wasn't something that he thought about except as it had to do with the way he would carve his Lucille angel. "She had more, uh, padding," he said. It didn't seem like enough of an answer. "Women weren't afraid to be women those days."

Lucille broke her pose and walked to the sink. She plugged the drain and squeezed Joy liquid over the dinner dishes. "What wife?" she asked.

The shoe man hadn't thought she'd heard him. "Angela."

"What a beautiful name," she whispered.

"For a beautiful girl." The shoe man found himself telling Lucille much more than he'd ever said out loud about his lost wife to any soul on this earth.

At the end of his story, Lucille held his hand as it rested

on the kitchen table. "To love so much . . . Is that her powder puff in the bedroom?"

The shoe man nodded yes. Mrs. Rice wouldn't have minded his whitest of possible lies. And Leopoldine? She was somewhere elsewhere. It might have been Angela's. Even Angela might have mistaken it for hers. He didn't want to admit how few mementos he had.

"Is it her in those pictures you have over there?" The shoe man might have said yes to that too, but he didn't. That was too far to go. He said nothing. "You must have a wedding picture?" The shoe man shrugged.

That night, as he lay under his angels thinking maybe he had enough sketches to start roughing out his Lucille's form on a block of wood, he remembered something long forgotten. Angela's father had had a connection at the *Eagle*. Though he had given the cops his copy and never gotten it back, there had been a picture in the *Eagle*, a picture and an announcement of their marriage.

Anyone who thinks he met this recollection with eager, unreserved joy had better think again along the lines of Pandora's box. Poor Pandora didn't come onto the earth unfettered. Remember, Zeus made her in revenge for being cheated at the sacrificial altar. So there was already a catch. When she was given a gift from the gods, a box and an order not to open it, it was no simple matter. All her traits, curiosity among them, were given to her by the most powerful of gods. What was she to do?

Should the shoe man wander three blocks to the library and check the microfilm? Such a trip was no simple matter, either, and he told himself he was no Pandora. He knew better than to make it in a hurry. Later, he decided, someday, tomorrow, in a week, in a month, when he was ready, whenever that was, he would go. Not a moment sooner. His decision gave him no peace. He couldn't dust his hands off and move on as if the days after this memory were the same as the days before. The possibility of seeing Angela's face once again taunted him, haunted him. First he would ask himself, What could be the harm? Then he would ask himself, What would be the point? Unlike poor curious Pandora, he knew what he would find. It wasn't the finding that frightened him. It was that he did not and could not know what it would mean.

Jack kept mum about his quandary, but Lucille noticed his discomfort. She asked if whatever was wrong was her fault. Though he answered quickly it was not, he believed it was. Had she not asked, he might not have remembered. He told her he had spring fever.

She took him at his word and said she had a cure. She baked robin's egg–blue-frosted chocolate cupcakes with multicolored sprinkles. She insisted they eat them together outside in the sunshine.

He did not consider blue a decent color for food. He did not consider food a cure. The cupcakes looked absurd to him and he was, for the first time, annoyed at his Lucille. Cupcakes. Couldn't she see beyond his answer to his heart? Cupcakes. What idiocy. She was the simplest soul he had ever met if she thought . . . The shoe man reconsidered his thoughts. He was, after all, a man with a secret room full of angels and even if Lucille was as simple as a daisy, he did not want to hurt her feelings. "And where is the sunniest spot?" he asked.

"I'll show you."

Lucille led him past the library to the botanical gardens. They sat on a carpet of pink petals that had fallen from the cherry trees. All around, the air was sweet but all the shoe man could think about was having to walk past the library a second time after their picnic was done. There was only so much a man could tolerate. Nearby, on a bench, the shoe man spotted an abandoned newspaper. It was the morning's *Post*. A good sign. A savings of forty cents. Lucille sprawled on the grass, caressing her face with the velvety petals. He paged through the paper. *"Some Like It Hot,"* he said.

"I like it just exactly like this," she answered.

"No, the movie. *Some Like It Hot*. Tonight on nine, at eight o'clock. With your Marilyn Monroe. Jack Lemmon. Tony Curtis. 'Don't miss this comedy classic,' " he read.

"Wow! My first Marilyn," she said, twisting on her side,

her small breasts pointing to the cloudless sky as she squinted to see if her cupcakes had taken effect. "Happy now?"

His deep wrinkles stretched into little pink rivers across his browned face as he smiled. "Yes," he answered truthfully.

They ate an early supper and after that, Lucille devoured her first delicious Marilyn, jiggle by wiggle by giggle. Her delight was his. For the hours he was sitting beside her on the double bed with a bowl of popcorn between them, the shoe man's cobwebbed heartaches seemed to belong to another man, not him. He thanked the powers that had brought him happiness at his age. He thanked the powers that had brought him Lucille.

During the commercials, she leaned her head on his shoulder. Lucille was so close, a strand of her white-blonde hair tickled his cheek and he brushed it gently away with his finger. Seeing the black polish stains that had become a part of his hands, she noticed the unlikely elegance of his fingers. And the strength. She liked men with strong hands. She hadn't thought about the shoe man's manliness until just then. Sitting beside him in his double bed, she was as happy, happy without trying, as she'd ever been. She knew he would never ask of her what other men asked. He wouldn't hurt her. He wouldn't leave her. He wouldn't tell her how he needed her then tell her what she lacked. Someday, she thought, she might, she just might kiss him. Someday, on the lips. She might, someday, stroke the stubble on his face, touch the grey curls on his chest, slide his T-shirt over his head, slide his green work trousers to the floor, take him into his own bed and give him all her best and everything, everything he would never ask for. All wrapped up with a bow. Maybe.

And then the commercials were over. The movie returned to the screen. The thought of being the shoe man's lover flew away as quickly as it had lighted. "You're barking up the wrong fish," said the uncomfortable He who was being taken for a very desirable She.

"Barking up the wrong fish," Lucille repeated. "I love it!"

THE END OF AN IDYLL

In its own way, the life Lucille and Jack lived together suited them both almost perfectly.

If only things had stayed just as they were.

If only the shoe man hadn't ended the evening with the comment that Lucille really did look like Marilyn, in a way.

If only she hadn't run to the mirror to see if what he was saying was so.

If only.

If only Lucille hadn't had a magnetic way of listening as if what he said, whatever it was, was the most important thing she could ever want to hear.

If only the rarity of being listened to so ardently hadn't

loosened the shoe man's longtime habit of keeping his thoughts stored safe in his head.

If only she hadn't brought up his wife again.

If only he hadn't mentioned the *Eagle* and mused to Lucille about whether Angela's face in the picture would be the face he thought he remembered so well.

If only.

If only the Yemenites hadn't had all their copies of the *Post* swiped off the shelf by thieves at dawn.

If only the shoe man had decided not to read the paper that day instead of buying the *News*.

If only he hadn't seen the ad for Hannigan's Steak and Brew Marilyn Monroe Look Alike Contest with cash prizes.

If only he hadn't brought it home to Lucille and said, "Why not?"

If only his encouragement hadn't meant so much to her.

If only the shoe man hadn't sensed that because of his own words and the way they were heard, he might yet lose his Lucille again, this time for real.

If only Lucille had lost her nerve.

If only he hadn't rushed to carve a heavy block of ash into an airy opal-eyed angel, the angel that would expose his perishable soul to the twisted truths of the printed word and the lie of the camera.

If only they'd never known Buddy Lomax.

Ah, if only.

THE CONTEST

Buddy Lomax didn't happen into Hannigan's to eat one of their shoeleather steaks. He sat alone with his camera and a plate of radishes beside him on the spotty green tablecloth. The radishes were tart. When he bit in, they bit back. He was prepared to be bored. He'd been to enough of these things to last other men two lifetimes, but he had reason to be patient. He knew what he was looking for. More precisely, he knew he'd know it if and when he found it. And she would be worth the wait once he finished with her. He checked his watch and walked to the salad bar to refill his plate. He bet himself the contest would start with "Diamonds Are a Girl's Best Friend." These things always did. And it did start with that, played through faulty speakers so that Marilyn's whisper sounded like rough water wearing down rocks in a stream. A white spotlight flooded the cleared away section of the dining room that had been made into a stage. Fifteen minutes late. Buddy felt a hopefulness that was probably unwarranted, but fifteen minutes late was better than the average and at least the spotlight wasn't red. Red was a disguise, hid the flaws. If you couldn't see what you were getting, you made mistakes, wasted time. Buddy Lomax pushed a radish into his cheek and watched. He counted eleven contestants waiting in a half moon formation beside the busboy's cart. Not much of a turnout. They either wore something like Marilyn's white halter dress from *The Seven Year Itch,* or your basic tight sequined gown and some fluffy fake fur. Some of the entrants hadn't even bothered to wear a wig. There were two chubby brownettes. On their first promenade under the light, Buddy spotted no probables, but because he was in a generous mood, he allowed to himself that there might be two or three possibilities.

Lucille was not among them.

Lucille had divided her day between her preparations and the shoe man's. She touched up her roots, waxed the hair off her legs and whipped egg whites into a mask, which she spread over her face. As the egg whites hardened, she rested with cucumber slices over her eyes and then she took the shoe man's one suit jacket to the speedy cleaners. She looked through his ties. They were dusty and out of style. She bought a carnation-printed tie from the street vendor who sold sunglasses and visors. One hundred percent silk for only five bucks. She returned home and bathed for an hour. After her bath, she baby-oiled her wet skin and rested again on the shoe man's double bed. Then she rushed to the cleaners for the shoe man's jacket and hurried him into closing the doors of Reliable a half hour early. She supervised the shoe man as he dressed. He balked at the tie. Hadn't worn one since Angela's parents' anniversary party forty years before. Lucille pleaded, and he let her do the knot. When he looked the way she wanted him to look, she left him in the kitchen with a cup of coffee and disappeared into the bathroom for two hours.

The shoe man fidgeted with Mrs. Rice's photographs until Lucille emerged all painted and coiffed and snapped into the thirty-dollar sequined sheath she'd found at the Cuban jumble shop. The shoe man barely knew her. "Oh my God," he said. "You're a shoo-in."

"You think?" said Lucille. She practiced a Marilyn pucker.

"Unless they're a bunch of potato-eyed louts."

The shoe man sat by the judges' table. He could tell it was the judges' table because five overweight men sat side by side and nobody sat across. Each man had his own pitcher of brew and his own yellow legal pad. The shoe man craned to see what they were writing, but he couldn't.

Lucille knew she was much more Marilyn than the brow-nette to her left, and the tall blonde on her right was a little too angular. The shoe man winked at her. She winked at the judges. One of them made a notation and she heard the blood pulse in her ears.

The first contestant was asked to give her name. "Mari-lyn," she said. Lucille thought it was coincidence. She was too nervous to listen to the rest of the girls, to realize that they were all called Marilyn and that that should be her name, too.

When she stepped forward and the manager said, "And your name is . . ." Lucille answered, "Lucille Bixby," and the candles on the restaurant tables flickered as the patrons, all of them except the shoe man, expelled gusts of laughter wind. I'm dead, she thought. It's all over. She covered her shame with a Marilyn smile.

It was the smile and not the gaffe that made Buddy Lomax notice her. He'd seen a lot of phony Marilyns at-tempt their version of her smile. Some of them came close, but close was not close enough. Lucille's smile was not a version. It wasn't hers at all. It was Marilyn's. Marilyn Monroe's coveted, inimitable smile was being smiled tonight at Hannigan's Steak and Brew. There she is, he thought, Coca-Cola. The Real Thing. Buddy ordered his mind to slow down. Smile aside, she was far from perfect. Her nose was off, her breasts were a bit puny, her waist too much of a chunk, and for some damn reason she had brown eyes. He would have to see her up close. Until then, this far he would go: Lucille Bixby was now a possible, and possibly a probable.

The judges didn't see it that way. The red roses and the bottle of Champagne and the five hundred dollars went to Marilyn number six.

Buddy crunched a radish. The judgment of the judges was pathetic. These five horny wedding-ringed poohbahs had chosen a man. Robert Smythe pronounced the *y* in his name. He did the circuit. And yes, he was the best of the Marilyn transvestites, but Marilyn Monroe had never had a penis, and although Robert had transformed almost every aspect of himself to conform to Marilyn's specs, he had not been willing to lose his dick.

Noting that one of the judges was already sliding his fingers down Robert's back, Buddy strung his camera around his neck and stuffed a radish in his shirt pocket. The losers had dispersed, some to change in the bathroom, some to sit with their friends. Some old man was ordering a drink for the girl with the smile. Assessing the old man, Buddy saw no threat. The old man didn't look rich enough to buy the love of a girl one third his age, yet there was something between them. The old man was patting her shoulder. Her head hung close to his mouth. Buddy corralled the waiter and paid for their beers. "You don't mind," he said as he joined the shoe man and Lucille at their table. The shoe man did mind, but he didn't say so. "Congratulations," Buddy continued.

"Hate to break it to you, but I lost," said Lucille.

"You were still the best," said the shoe man.

Buddy drew a line through the frost on his mug. "You could be better."

"Who asked you?" the shoe man grumbled. He was angry now. His cheeks tingled. He brought the mug to his mouth and fantasized about punching the words back into this wiseguy's kisser.

"How?" said Lucille. "The girl who won . . ."

"That was a man."

Lucille twisted in her seat to get a look at Marilyn number six. "That's not a man. I lost to a man?"

"It's getting late," said the shoe man.

"Just a sec." Lucille took her hand from the shoe man's arm and leaned toward the stranger. "So, how?"

Buddy smiled. He saw the wanting in her face. The rare need Marilyn had had. There was even more here than he had hoped for. "For one thing, the brown eyes. If you're going to be doing this Marilyn thing, why don't you at least get yourself a pair of contacts?"

"These are contacts."

"Marilyn's eyes weren't brown."

"But in all the pictures . . ."

"Then you're looking at the wrong pictures."

"It's almost one in the morning."

Buddy removed a business card from his wallet. "Your father wants to get going."

Her father. What did this stranger know? "What makes you think . . ."

"This is Jack," said Lucille, in a way that made it clear to Buddy that father or not, she wanted to hear what he had to say. "And I'm Lucille."

"Buddy Lomax." Laying his hand over hers, he placed his card in her palm. He stood. "If you want to be the best, much better than Robert over there, it's not enough to just look like Marilyn. It's not even enough to have her smile, which you do . . ."

"I do?"

"Yes, you do. It's not enough. Imitation is always second-rate. And when it comes to Marilyn, you've got every other lunatic dressing up in costume, pretending. If they went around acting like Napoleon, they'd be in the bin, but with Marilyn, no. It's open season. And it's all bull. If you want to be Marilyn, you have to *be* her. I know." Buddy also knew how to make an exit that guaranteed his next entrance. He kissed Lucille's hand. No one had ever done that.

"What a snake," said the shoe man.

"Oh, I thought he was nice," said Lucille.

The late hour made it easy for the shoe man and Lucille

to end their conversation at that point. Buddy's card stayed in Lucille's palm all the way back to Brooklyn. By the time she was alone in the bathroom, the card was molded to her hand.

Buddy Lomax. Image Banker. Buddy made her forget that she hadn't won the prize. It wasn't that he was handsome. His hips were wider than his shoulders, his hair was unnaturally shiny, his upper lip was rounded and his lower lip was thin, but he would help her. He knew how. He said so and she could tell he was telling the truth. She made some promises to herself and then she fell asleep.

Locked in his angel room, the shoe man stripped down to his shorts and lay on the couch. He closed his eyes. It was too hot. He opened the window and closed his eyes again. No good. In a silent bull fury, he gave up on his sleep and attacked the pristine ash block with a charcoal pencil. In spite of the hour, he slashed the lines away with his knife. White splinters fell to the floor. The planes of Lucille's face began to emerge from the wood. Her head sat well on her uncarved shoulders. He stood back, seeing more than was actually there. He imagined the base of her wings as they joined the spine and how they would reach out, spanning maybe ten feet. He would make the wings from rich-colored hardwoods. As he dreamt of what the angel would become under his hands, night became day and although he didn't remember falling asleep, he woke to the smell of fresh strawberry muffins.

What the shoe man didn't know was that when Lucille had gone to the Koreans for fresh strawberries and while she was out and away from him, she had stopped at the phone booth on the corner and called Buddy Lomax.

What the shoe man didn't know, Lucille didn't tell him.

he restaurant was nothing special. The sun was high and after they ate, they stepped into the shade so Buddy could take a few pictures of Lucille, nothing spicy, nothing nude, just snapshots on the street. Looking through the lens, he said, "I see real potentiality here."

Lucille said, "Thanks." She didn't ask what exactly he meant or what an image banker was. She didn't ask straight out for lots of Marilyn tips. She didn't want to seem too ignorant so she didn't say very much at all.

Buddy walked her to the subway and kissed her on the forehead when she'd expected a kiss on the lips. She left feeling a failure. Why hadn't he kissed her on the lips? As she rode the train, she thought about her future and decided that the most important thing about her first date with Buddy Lomax was that it would lead to the second and she would try harder to be irresistible. Without having to ask, she knew Buddy Lomax wouldn't waste the film in his camera on a girl who didn't strive.

Lucille stayed on the train one stop beyond Reliable Repair. She wanted to bring Jack a present, something wonderful to make up for the secret she was keeping from him. She whirled through the revolving door of the Brooklyn Public Library and almost whirled out again. She hadn't been in a public library, ever. Books crammed with little black letters weren't for her. The books in her mother's house, the Bible, the *Joy of Cooking,* were so dusty they made her sneeze. Thinking of the potentiality Buddy said she had, she made herself stay and put it to use. She asked where to find the old *Eagle*s. She expected a pile of papers. Instead, a man in a yellow sweater led her to a machine and stuck a black thingamajig on a silvery post and switched on a motor. "Turn this," he said, and he walked away.

Lucille stared at the machine. It wasn't for her. She pushed back her chair and searched for the man in the yellow sweater. "Excuse me," she said, "but do you think you could help?" She offered her widest Marilyn smile and leaned forward slightly, pressing her arms against her ribs to make the most of her cleavage.

The man in the yellow sweater was a librarian. He collected a meager paycheck. After Social Security, the union, health benefits and the government, there was little left for luxuries. Even in his youth he had not been the sort of a man pretty young girls seduced, but there was always a dream and a chance, wasn't there?

On behalf of the dream and the chance, he spooled through a hundred weeks' worth of the microfilm. Lucille bent alluringly over his shoulder, marveling at his speed and prowess.

"Wow," she murmured.

And then he found just what she thought Jack wanted, a picture of his Angela. She hadn't realized the photo would be backward.

"How come it's like that?"

"It's a negative image," said the man.

"Oh," said Lucille.

From her tone, the man in the yellow sweater knew that his chances had vanished. "I'd best get back to work," he said.

Lucille forgot to thank him. Hoping that backward was better than nothing, she slid two dimes and a nickel into the slot at the side of the machine and waited for a black face, white hair, black eyes, white lips negative print of the shoe man's beaming beloved lost bride.

Lucille was so excited she walked from the library to Reliable Repair just to tell the shoe man she had a surprise and she wasn't going to tell him what it was. Then she winked and waved and went shopping.

When the shoe man got home that evening, Lucille hid her hands behind her back.

"Come on," said the shoe man. "Let's have it."

"Pretty please?"

"First I put on a tie, then she wants me to say pretty please."

Lucille saw the logic in his argument. She handed Jack a rolled page of shiny paper. Because she was watching his face for joy as the shoe man unrolled the paper, she didn't understand what she saw instead. First he turned red, then he turned white. The shoe man stared at the shadows that composed a flat version of something like Angela at nineteen. His groin burned and he gasped at the sudden heat. It wasn't desire. Something else, more than grief, other than fear, made the shoe man have to think to breathe when seconds before his breath had come naturally. "Why," he asked, "did you bring me this?"

"Isn't that her?"

"Yes, it is."

"Well, I thought . . ." Lucille stopped.

If this was what came of thinking, thought the shoe man, I never want it done in my presence again. He dared to look at Lucille. She was hurt. Hurt that he wasn't happy to hold this ghost in his hand after he, himself, had resisted tempta-

93

tion. "You don't know what this means to me, Lucille," he said, adding, "Thank you," for her sake.

If only, instead of pretending gratitude, the shoe man had looked at Angela's reversed image once and thrown it away in a trash can on the street. If only.

He carried the image from the kitchen to the bathroom, from the bathroom to the back room, not knowing where or how to put it down. He wanted not to look at it, not to wonder and remember, but it was too late. He opened drawers and closed them with Angela's bridal picture still in his hand.

Hell is not only a place or a condition, it is a machine. More specifically, it is a computer manufactured by Linotype Hell Graphics, of Hauppauge, Long Island, that breaks down pictures into minuscule dots that correspond to numbers and then manipulates the numbers and dots to make other pictures. As a Hell technician, Buddy made good money, but he never got a chance to go beyond the mundane. At least not on Agency time. The Agency had him using the Hell to do things like taking a photo of a model with a lovely face and giving her a better body and then taking the merged, better model, giving her brown hair blonde streaks and putting her, say, on a sandy beach in the Bahamas against date palms from Palm Springs in front of a blue sky seen and shot in Kenya and then making the blue even bluer so that consumers would buy the client's better brand of soft drink. No one at The Agency gave a damn past the client's wishes. Buddy Helled what he was told to Hell. Sometimes six equally important people would sit behind him as he worked the controls, shouting across each other as they rocketed their differing opinions off the padded walls and into his ears. Buddy Lomax was as rare as a black diamond. Every one of them would leave the room content that his or her will had been done. Though they never saw beyond the back of his head, Buddy pleased them all. Never had a complaint about his work. Got his raises on schedule, but.

But. He was angry, as livid as a man who pleases everyone can be. His vision exceeded that of the two-dimensional Agency minds to whom he kowtowed every working day. Knowing all the Hell could do made him its master. Knowing its limitations, he dreamt of possibilities, of taking true moments and turning them into moments that never were. He tinkered, customized the Agency Hell, transcending the limits of the maker's design. His could do more. His could do better. Knowing what *his* Hell could do wasn't enough. He dreamt of exceeding mere simulation and making new truths that were truer than those of which they were composed, of showing those Agency know-nothings what could be known, what could be done by Buddy Lomax, alone. He dreamt of surpassing the Hell's capabilities with his own hands and mind, doing what it could do, only more, only better, in three dimensions, not a measly two, with a live image, the new Marilyn, *his* Marilyn, his creation. And who was to say he couldn't?

But first he had to secure the girl. He stayed at the machine through lunch to prepare. What he had in mind was a simple, seductive transformation, something to show her why she should be his. It wouldn't take much. She was so full of wanting. She was almost his without trying. He could do what needed to be done this first time in an hour. He knew Lucille would be easily impressed. And she was.

At five, Lucille met Buddy at one of the fancy McDonald's she'd heard about but never been in, one of the ones with flowers on the table and espresso in hard plastic cups with tiny handles. They ordered, and as soon as they'd divvied up the fries, Buddy removed an envelope from his breast pocket and slid it across the table. Lucille could tell this envelope held something magnificent. She wiped her fingers clean. "Should I open it?"

"Can you not?"

"No." She tore open the flap. There were four photographs. "These are from the other day," she said without looking.

"Look," Buddy answered.

"Wow." There she was in Paris, France, when she'd never

been in Paris, France. There she was waving from a bateau mouche on the Seine. There she was arm in arm with Buddy in front of the Eiffel Tower. There she was standing in the Louvre beside the Mona Lisa. "How'd you do this?"

"Presto, change-o," he said.

Lucille knew a picture never lied. She doubted what she held in her hand and then she doubted herself. "But I was never there, I don't think."

"Maybe someday you will be."

"Yeah, but . . ." Why should she go to Paris if she already had the snapshots? Paris had always been her first choice. Maybe then it would be Rome. She decided not to tell Buddy she wanted to go to Rome. He might put her there. Lucille chewed her Marilyn-red lower lip in a very un-Marilyn way. What was there after Paris and Rome? London. She wondered if Buddy could put her with Prince Charles or the Pet Shop Boys.

"Hush." He meant, Don't think, don't speak. "Don't distort yourself."

"Wow," said Lucille. Then he kissed her, leaning over the table just like in the movies. It wasn't the best kiss she'd ever had, but it was Buddy's kiss, and she acted the difference between how she felt and how she thought she ought to feel.

"Pretty passionate," he commented as they cleared their trays.

"Is that good or bad?" asked Lucille. Buddy didn't answer. She followed him out, saying nothing when he led her to his apartment. On the walls, there were photos of Marilyn. Not a few, a few dozen, all in gold frames. Floor to ceiling bookshelves flanked the door to his bedroom. "Wow, you really like to read."

"Never touch those."

Lucille stepped closer to examine the bindings of the forbidden books. *Finding Marilyn: A Romance; The Secret Happiness of Marilyn Monroe; The Agony of Marilyn Monroe; The Marilyn Monroe Story; Norma Jean: The Life of Marilyn Monroe; Legend: The Life and Death of Marilyn Monroe; Diary of a Lover of Marilyn Monroe; Marilyn Monroe: A Life on Film; Will Acting Spoil Marilyn Monroe?; The Films of Marilyn Monroe; Conversations with Marilyn; Marilyn Monroe Confidential; Marilyn Monroe: A Composite View; Marilyn: The Tragic Venus; The Story of Marilyn Monroe; Monroe: Her Life in Pictures; The Last Sitting; The Story of the Misfits; The Life and Curious Death of Marilyn Monroe; The Strange Death of Marilyn Monroe; The Mysterious Death of Marilyn Monroe; Marilyn Monroe: Murder Cover-Up; Who Killed Marilyn?; The Marilyn Conspiracy; Marilyn Monroe; Marilyn Monroe; Marilyn; Marilyn; Marilyn; Goddess.*

"Why?"

It was crucial that she not become another tedious student of Marilyn's miserable life. "Anything you need to know, I will tell you." Buddy walked through the doorway. Lucille followed. Buddy sat on the red spread that covered his king-size bed. Lucille sat beside him. "No, stand," he said. "Undress."

Lucille did as she was told, undoing her blouse a button at a time, checking his eyes for approval, his trousers for arousal, and finding little of either. Buddy just watched, saying nothing. Lucille's fingers became more awkward. She undid the waistband of her skirt. It dropped in a heap, encircling her ankles. She stepped away from it and blushed. She was wearing pantyhose. "I should have worn garters or something, right?"

"Garters are good," Buddy answered, leaning back on his elbows.

Lucille smiled. "Next time."

"We'll take care of all that," he said.

Lucille kicked her shoes off her feet and wriggled out of her underpants. "I don't have anything else to take off," she said when Buddy made no move to touch her.

"You feel naked."

"Well, you're staring at me. You're not *doing* anything."

"Yes. Does it excite you?"

"Well, actually . . ." Lucille wanted to give the right answer but she didn't know what it was so she told the truth. "It kind of gives me the creeps."

"That will have to change," said Buddy. Then he stood.

His touch, first denied, was now bestowed as he measured her waist with his hands to determine the needed reduction. He examined the dimples in her buttocks, which were charming, though the buttocks could be rounder. The cleft and the curve of her back were sublime. He touched her, and Lucille felt relief, then gratitude that rose to an intolerable fever. "Yes," he said, more to himself than Lucille. "My little Marilyn." He placed his mouth over the tip of her breast and nibbled at her nipple until it stood erect. He pinched the other to the same state and stepped back to admire the symmetry. He opened the petals of her vagina and bent to inspect, but at the touch of his lips, before his tongue had reached its tiny destination, Lucille shuddered and collapsed in orgasm. "Aren't we eager." He dipped his finger into the wet depth and felt the pulsing all around it. "Aren't we the lucky girl." Oblivious to the critical chill in his tone, not knowing anything but her need to have Buddy inside her, she reached for him. He pulled away. He didn't want Lucille. He wanted Marilyn, and until everything was as it should be, he could do without. Still, it would be a bother to explain, explanation could only muddy up matters. It was best to go through with it. He removed nothing. Unzipping his fly, he slid his penis through his briefs. Lucille was startled to find it limp. She coaxed him to readiness with gentle fingers, and as soon as Buddy could manage, he had her hard and short. He expelled his climax with a grunt and pulled back again. "So," he said. "I can see we're not frigid."

Lucille grinned and nuzzled her head against the grey-brown fuzz on his shoulder. "Nope."

Buddy dabbed the semen off his penis with a peach-colored tissue. "Lesson begins." Buddy lifted Lucille's hair off the back of her neck and caressed the revealed space sweetly. He wrapped a sheltering arm around her and stroked her face. "Are you absolutely sure about this Marilyn business, little one? Are you ready to make sacrifices?"

"Yes," Lucille answered absolutely.

"The first is the biggest."

"What?"

"Well, when we think of Marilyn, what do we think of? What makes a man want her thirty years after she's dead? Sex. And I don't mean fireworks. I mean promise. And it's a funny thing about sex in the promise department, little one. It's gotta be unfulfilled. She's gotta have it, and he's gotta want it. And she, I mean Marilyn, you, gotta love love love to be looked at, up and down, make it all count, every inch of your pretty little self. But. And here's the secret. Here's the part they don't get, the second-raters. Marilyn's whole allure thing, sewing her ass into dresses, no panties— no more panties for you, by the way—all of that hot tamale stuff, Kennedys dropping like flies, and guess what? She couldn't come her way out of a paper bag. See? I heard folks who said she could, but they were lying. A satisfied woman doesn't knock herself out trying to sex up every man she sees. She knows she's got it even if she ain't getting it, if you know what I mean. But if you can't . . . well then you got a special need and you work at it and you worry about it and it drives you. Keep trying to reel 'em in to prove you've got what you don't have."

"Huh?"

"What I'm sayin' is, no more lollapaloozas for you, period. Starting tomorrow, 'cause today is a waste, I'm not gonna let you come, now or ever. You save that all for the camera, little one, and you're going to be the greatest," he told her. Buddy stopped her disbelieving giggle with an excited kiss on her Marilyn mouth that made Lucille desperate for air. She tore away, gasping. "You save that up. Now get dressed."

Buddy threw the lace bikini panties she'd bought to make herself more irresistible in with the carrot peels under his sink and gave her money for cab fare, but she put it in her purse and took the subway. She wanted to ride in a tin can and think, but she was muscle weary and baffled and she had climaxed so completely that all she could do was half close her eyes and listen as the conductor made garbled announcements over the loudspeaker.

hile Lucille was being seduced, if what was happening to her could be called seduction, the shoe man carved. A light breeze drove off the day's heat. With the soothing air came the loud, buzzing bumpadumpabumpa of radio music, if what he was hearing could be called music. He hacked to the rhythm and he made fast progress. He knew where Lucille was. She hadn't told him. He just knew. In time, the radios went indoors with their owners and the shoe man heard the low horns of tankers and garbage barges edging between the banks of the East River. He unpacked his delicate tools and turned to the finer work. From the sketches, he shaped the bridge of her nose with its particular little knob at the end. After he refined her brow,

the shoe man matched and sanded the small hills that sloped
to her eye sockets. He roughed the outline of her lids, but
because it involved the setting of jewels, the shoe man always saved the eyes themselves until after an angel's color-
ing had set. Using diamond-dust sandpaper, he polished her
cheeks until they were softer than human skin. He pulled a
stool close to her face and donned a pair of magnifying
bifocals he'd purchased from the Hasid who sold him stones.
Steadying his elbow against the jagged block that was yet to
become her body, the shoe man stared at the rectangular rise
of wood that was to become her lips. Should she be smiling
as wide as a half moon, he wondered, or thoughtful? Should
he try to show the quiver that drew in one side of her lower
lip when she was unsure? He did not know. Leaning his face
against his angel, he closed his eyes to think. That was no
good. He thought about Lucille and what she might be
doing. He thought about Angela and Angela's reverse picture. And where was the picture? Under the sketches. He'd
buried it, pretending it was lost. He knew he ought to lay the
sketches side by side to study the curves of Lucille's mouth,
but he was in no mood for uncovering, not now. He heard
sirens come deafeningly close and wondered where the fire
was. His windows were open. There was no smoke. He assumed he was safe and leaned out for air.

He saw the mass murderer at play in the moonlight,
taunting two hungry stray cats with a scrap of meat. The

animals yowled and the shoe man cursed and slammed the window shut. The beastly cries escalated to unbearability. The shoe man opened his window once again and yelled, "Cut it out," but over the yeowwowhiss, the mass murderer's laugh and the scuffling, he couldn't hear his own voice. Hoping to disperse the cats, he tossed a scrap of ash toward the fracas. There was one startling second of silence, and then the mass murderer's infernal delight as the cats went at it again. The shoe man turned back to his angel. He tried to deafen himself with the work. His hands were unsteady with anger. Even the broadest cuts wobbled. His concentration had been shot straight to hell.

ucille heard the stuttering shots, but they didn't frighten her. She assumed they were just the usual M-80 firecrackers. Though it was weeks 'til the Fourth, city kids started early, launching loud explosives and sparkling whizzing whirling lights from the rooftops. She looked up. The moon was missing. An airplane's red and white flashing lights crossed the sky. As her eyes followed, she was knocked hard to her knees by three running schoolboys. She yelped. One of the boys stopped and, panting, he hovered over her. His shiny brown face reflected yellow light from the street lamp. He reached into his Teenage Mutant Ninja Turtles book bag. Lucille waited to be robbed. Robbed before dawn by a ten-year-old with a book bag and his cute little friends.

One of the other two said, "Shit, man, fuck, shit, come on, we're in deep shit, man, we're gonna git our asses fucked." The children vanished into the dark.

The sidewalk had shaved off a layer of skin. She sat watching little bloody beads travel down her shinbone. "Filthy-mouthed little bastards ought to be in bed," she grumbled.

She was still dabbing at her scrapes when she saw more cop cars than she'd ever seen in one place book-end the block. Windows lit up both sides of the street. Someone must have heard her scream.

She marveled at the response as she rehearsed her embarrassed thanks. It's really just a little cut. You're too kind, really. Really, it's nothing.

A roaring ambulance cut through the blockade and did not stop for her. Lucille waited for the driver to realize he'd overshot his mark. The ambulance braked. When she saw where, she put away her fantasies, pulled herself to her feet and ran toward it fearing it had come for Jack. A gang of men leapt out the back, pulling rubber gloves over their hands. Pushing past the police, Lucille shoved her way forward. When the rubber-gloved men reappeared, the rush was over. They carried a stretcher. It was covered with a sheet and the sheet was black with spreading blood that dribbled off the sides into the last of the night. She dug her nails into an officer's arm. "Oh, God," she cried, blaming herself for not having been home. And then she saw that the cops were clustered at the door of the old house next door.

"Shooting," the cop answered without having been asked.

"Who?"

"Likely name of Heinz. Someone Heinz. Know him?"

Lucille shook. She heard herself laugh and covered her mouth to pretend a sob. Here a man was dead and she was laughing. Her relief was greater than her horror. It wasn't Jack. "No," said Lucille.

She expected to meet Jack in the growing crowd that filled the street. He wasn't there. Eager to discuss the shooting, she unlocked the door. There was no light in the hall. There was no light in the bathroom. The kitchen was dark, and no light drifted under the closed door to his back room. She pressed her ear against the wood and heard his loud, steady breathing. "Jack?" she tested. He didn't answer.

By the time she opened her eyes, Jack was dressed and on his second cup of coffee. "Late night," was all he said when she wandered out of her room wrapped in his seersucker robe.

"Do you know anyone named Heinz?" asked Lucille.

"No," Jack answered, pulling out a chair so she could sit.

"Well, he's dead. Shot."

"Shame," said the shoe man as he ate his banana muffin. "What a shame."

he police had festooned the garden fence with yellow tape printed with a fierce legal warning, but the neighborhood cats didn't know how to read and six or seven happy strays were sunning alongside the toppled statue of Quetzalcoatl as if nothing at all had happened. Because the mass murderer hadn't tended the garden with the tenderness toward plants and earth that old Mrs. Rice had shown, the soil out back was hungry and drank all the blood that was spilled on it. On the slate steps leading from the front door to the street, however, deep red splatters led to wide red seas, marking the speed with which the body had rid itself of life.

Officers Ullman and Couch strolled Flatbush with cups of

café con leche in hand, waiting for gossip to travel, looking, they knew not for what. The garden had offered scant evidence. Most of the neighbors had ignored the shots. The bullets had entered from a baffling angle. There were paw prints everywhere, but no complete footprints or fingerprints except those of the dead Mr. Heinz. The hideous statue that had smashed Heinz's head as he fell was astonishingly bloodless and all they had to carry away was a triangular scrap of white wood that somehow didn't belong.

Officer Ullman found six passport photos of Heinz atop the fireplace mantel. He had one in his shirt pocket.

When he showed it to Gloria the pizza lady, she betrayed her old friend casually, chat chat chatting him into a quagmire. Yes, of course she had seen that man. He ordered vegetarian pizza and left the crust. No, she didn't know his name, but everybody called him the mass murderer. He lived next door to the shoe man at the corner. Who was everybody? Everybody. The shoe man? Yes, the shoe man called him the mass murderer, too. And why was he called the mass murderer? No reason, really. He looked like one, that's all. Did he have any enemies? How should she know? Could she think of any reason anyone would want to kill him? No, but the shoe man wanted to shoot out a couple statues. One of those gods, like in *National Geographic*. Aztec, Egyptian, a death god, real ugly. And a dog on a tree.

A what? Ask him, he's the one who wanted the gun, she said, and then made matters worse by slapping her hand to her mouth as she realized what she had done.

Gloria was glad the Albanians were late to work and didn't hear.

By the time Vic sauntered in with his pit bulls, her memory had reshaped the conversation so that she didn't look so bad to herself.

"The police were in," she said to the shoe man when he ordered his calzone.

"They came by me, too," he answered. "Heinz. Shame. Can't say I'll miss him. Too bad. Wonder if he was any relation to the ketchup."

"Yeah."

"Asked a hell of a lot of questions."

"To me, too."

"My friend Lucille saw him carried out on a stretcher. Lots of blood."

"Your friend Lucille." Gloria pushed her hair behind one ear and grinned like the toothy wolf who met Red Riding Hood in the woods. "A blondie. Natural? Very pretty. Do you know James Mason once saw me on a sidewalk and invited me to a, what do they call it? Screen test. I didn't go."

"Had something better to do," drawled Vic.

"I wouldn'ta gone with you if I was a star, you better

believe . . ." Gloria returned her attention to the shoe man. She glanced quickly at the crotch of his baggy chinos. Maybe he was hung like a racehorse and she'd missed it all these years. "So, what is it with you and that girl, anyway? She's how old? Very young . . ."

The shoe man stared at his greasy napkin. "Nothing."

"I see." Gloria didn't hide her pique. If he was keeping the girl a secret, who knew what other secrets he kept? "So who do you think killed the mass murderer?"

"Could have been anyone."

Gloria scooped crushed ice into a large wax-covered paper cup and covered the ice with seltzer. She held her face above the fizz and felt the little bubbles explode. "Never know."

ucille dropped her salad tongs when the police buzzed the shoe man's intercom. She lifted her finger from the Talk button so they couldn't hear. "You don't have to let 'em in without a warrant," she said knowingly, whispering just in case the words snuck through somehow.

He pulled a cucumber from the bowl and ate a neat circle around the translucent seeds. "Let 'em up."

Lucille did as he asked, and his calm increased her fear. Neither the police nor the shoe man mentioned a warrant. Rather than speak to them at the door, the shoe man led Officers Ullman and Couch to the red-topped table and started a fresh pot of coffee in Mrs. Rice's percolator just for them. Lucille bustled around the kitchen, noisily setting the makings of dinner to the side as she tried to cover the nervous rumbling of her stomach. The shiny Formica reflected red on Officer Ullman's forearms as he stirred sugar into his cup. His stirring continued long after the sugar had dissolved, the silver spoon endlessly pinging the china over and over as, over the ping, his conversation rambled over the neighborhood and the neighbors and who did what and who lived where and so on with horrifying amiability. Lucille was distressed that Jack gave no sign of knowing that the seemingly aimless talk was pointed at him.

"Oh, I might of heard it and I might of not," he said. "You hear guns and what-nots all night long, you screen it out the way we used to screen out the crickets. Used to have crickets here in this neighborhood. And owls. Owl tried living here now he'd get lung cancer."

Ullman blew air out his nose. "So the neighborhood's gone bad."

"That's more than one man's opinion. But the grocery's better. Them Koreans know produce."

"What did you think of this Heinz? Think he was up to anything could end him up cold? Drugs? Women?"

"Like I said before, I don't want to speak ill of the dead but he didn't strike me as no prize, that's all I can say." Jack pushed his shoulders back and Lucille heard his spine crackle. "Here's one for you, though. Might of been a homo.

Wore a dress in the backyard, swear to God, a striped number. And he had lousy legs. Lousy legs. If a guy's gonna wear
a dress he ought to have legs." Jack laughed. "I don't know.
I don't want to speak ill." Jack paused. "So you say there
was no witnesses, huh?"

"None yet, why?"

"No particular. Tell 'em what you saw, Lucille."

Lucille scrutinized Officer Couch. While Ullman kept Jack
talking, Couch had drifted out of the kitchen. Then he'd
wandered into the bathroom. Stayed awhile with the door
closed and come out again without flushing. Then he'd
leaned with his back fitted to the bedroom doorway, pretending not to look in. Couch winked when he caught Lucille
eyeing him and she snapped her head away. "Nothing. You
looking for something?"

Ignoring her question, Couch rejoined his partner in the
kitchen. "Nice place," he said to Jack as he put his hand on
the doorknob leading to the back room and tried it. It was
locked. "You got a window or two back here?"

For the first time since Ullman and Couch had arrived,
Jack was uncomfortable. "Yeah."

"Looks out over Heinz's place?"

Jack scraped at the skin around his thumb until it curled
away and began to bleed. "More or less."

"Mind if I take a look?" said Couch.

The tinkle of Officer Ullman's spoon marked the length of

the shoe man's agitated silence. "It's kind of a mess back there," Jack lied. "I'd rather not."

"It'd be a lot of trouble to go back and get a warrant and then we'd have to come all the way back here which would be a real pain and I'd get off late and my wife hates for me to be late, if you know what I mean." Couch grinned, loving his power. Ullman stirred as he watched Jack suck the blood off his torn thumb. And the shoe man realized he had no choice.

Every part of him resisted. His body turned heavy, his muscles stiff. It took minutes to stand and minutes more to fish the depths of his pockets. Couch's impatient hand moved to cover his gun.

"If you want me to open the door I got to get out my keys. You want to shoot me for that?"

"Don't get cute. I don't like cute."

The shoe man felt the cool notches along the brass key. Maybe the key wouldn't open the door and the cops would kill him and say he tried to fight. Maybe when he opened the door he would find the angels had vanished. Maybe there never were any angels. Maybe the murderer's gun would be lying on the worn oak floor. Maybe the police weren't really there. Maybe his heart had stopped beating and he was already dead. Maybe this was hell.

Couch snapped his fingers. "Chop chop."

"Is that necessary?" Ullman muttered.

Lucille stared at the lock, unable to look directly at the shoe man, ashamed at the magnitude of her own curiosity and her eagerness to see behind the door.

WHAT THEY SAW

The shoe man turned the key and Lucille saw heaven almost as she had always imagined it to be. Golden, graceful, pure in color and beautiful beyond thought and words. All that was missing was God, God and clouds. Even the shoe man's couch and workbench, even Angela's faded curtains, seemed a part of heaven in this room. All-seeing sapphire-eyed angels, emerald-eyed angels on the brink of a fall, furious angels and angels of mercy, broad-shouldered onyx-eyed guardian angels and angels whose obsidian eyes absorbed the truth, ruby-eyed angels rejoicing, searching angels and angels with six heads, angels shaped like wheels and sorrowful angels weeping topaz tears, and among them, she saw herself half transformed. She felt her heart enter the wooden angel with her face.

Ullman saw a fortune's worth of jewels and wondered where the hell the shoe man got the money. Crossing himself respectfully before the heavenly host, he murmured, "Holy moly, what'd ya rob, the Vatican?"

Couch noticed all the knives. "Where do you keep your gun?" he asked as he inspected the blades.

The shoe man said nothing. His angels had been exposed. His naked soul had been mauled. He was well past words. In his shock, what could he say?

"Probably some cult," Couch continued as he walked to the window that was graced by the beatific Raphael. "Voo-doo? Santería? Satan?" Looking down into the night at the mass murderer's garden, Couch calculated angle and distance. "Clear shot from here," he told his partner.

"You accusing him?" demanded Lucille. "Well forget about it. He doesn't have no gun and besides, I was with him all last night. Posing. See?" She stood beside the ash-wood angel to prove the likeness.

She was lying, trying to save the shoe man. And her words were more painful than Couch's insinuation. He understood. She believed it was he who had killed the mass murderer. His voice was so low it might have been missed. "I didn't do it," he said.

"Nobody ever does it," said Couch.

Ullman put one hand on the shoe man's shoulder. "Listen," he said. "If I were you, uh . . ."

Lucille placed her cheek on the cool, smooth cheek of her likeness. Fear flowed blood hot through her body. Tugging at his sideburns, Couch stared until he saw not what she wanted him to see, but something damning. Ash wood. The white wood in the garden. He didn't bother to hide his pleasure. He wiped his finger across his slimy teeth and said, "Do yourself an eensy beensy favor. Don't leave town."

The shoe man hadn't left town since the brief Niagara Falls honeymoon he'd taken with Angela way back when and he didn't *not* leave town just because some swaggering cop named Couch had watched a few too many westerns. The shoe man knew what he had and had not done. He wasn't afraid of Couch's insinuations. Not much.

Lucille frightened him more. Oh, he still treasured her company and she needed him more than before, despite her unspoken suspicions and the shoe man's unspoken hurt. No. It was Lucille and the angels. For forty years his angels had been his, and his alone. Even Angela's angel, the one meant for a gift, had never been seen by anyone but its maker. Now the key had been turned. The door had been opened. And after Couch and Ullman had gone, Lucille remained.

She knocked on his door in the morning, bringing his coffee to him on the couch instead of serving at the red-topped table so that she might have an excuse to stand in the angel room as the early light brought their jeweled eyes alive and the morning breezes tickled their faces and hers.

Her love of his angels did not entirely please the shoe man. With her love came a sense of proprietorship. She called the angel with her face "my angel," and she meant it.

She made suggestions. *Suggestions!*

She offered to undress and pose so that his rendering of her body would be exact. Jack didn't know what to do. He was terrified. He was tempted to accept.

It became difficult to carve. She wanted to watch. He refused her. Still, even when he was alone with his tools in his hands, he knew he was no longer entirely in control of the work they did, he and his hands. He felt not only the angels about him but the weight of Lucille's enthusiasm. On the good days it slowed him. On the bad days carving became impossible and he would stare at the awful reversed photograph of his lost Angela knowing she had done this to him, that his predicament was all her fault.

If only she had stayed where she ought to have stayed, with her husband who knew he loved her more than any other man possibly could, there would never have been any wooden angel but the first. There would have been children and chicken pox, mortgage debt and memories and grand-children and retirement. If only.

The shoe man begged Lucille never to mention the angels to anyone else. She promised that easily. "They'll be our secret," said Lucille.

But the "our" was a problem. And so was the secret, though the shoe man didn't know it at the time.

Meanwhile, the police went on with their investigating. The truth did not reveal itself and they simply couldn't find it or enough of it to charge the shoe man or anyone else.

Yet.

The shoe man did what he had always done, tending to his customers and their worn soles, eating alternate lunches of pizza and spinach calzone at Gloria's. What else was there to do?

He learned to endure the bad days. He continued carving, however slowly, and came to the conclusion that the slowing down had a purpose of its own, for as he worked on his Lucille angel, Lucille continued to change. Had he worked at his normal pace, the angel would have borne less and less resemblance to its inspiration. Even as it was, it was hard to keep up.

LUCILLE'S REMARKABLE
MARILYNIZATION

Though Lucille had entwined herself ever more in his life and the life of his angels, the shoe man knew he was losing her. It was an elusive loss. Not the usual thing. It wasn't the same as losing Angela or Angie, Mrs. Rice or Leopoldine. And it had to do with Buddy. Naturally, the shoe man assumed Buddy and Lucille were lovers. When he pictured their loving, which he could not help doing, he pictured it in the way he knew, the way he and Angela had been together. After forty years, so many years, the touches, sighs, shudders were still imaginable to him, and when he imagined them, and Lucille, and Buddy, he found himself adding a second beer to his traditional nightly one. In his innocence, he imagined that someday Lucille and Buddy might marry and have a family. It took two beers not to think about it. But even after two beers he still thought about the main thing, the real loss.

Lucille was not Lucille anymore.

Lucille's Marilynization was along the lines of a living miracle, a miracle with frighteningly divine results, a miracle in which nothing divine was involved. He'd never seen anything like it. Though he called her Lucille and she answered to that name, she called herself Marilyn, and from what he could see and hear, she was practically right. She'd bought herself another pair of contacts, blue-grey this time. The exact shade, the right shade, according to Buddy. Under Buddy's tutelage, her voice had evolved into a sugar-crisp whisper. The way she walked was different. It wasn't a walk anymore. It was a white ship at sea. It was a rolling wave. The cherished feeling that he might be her father or even her grandfather curled in and browned at the edges, tainted by self-disgust and confusion. How could his gut not go tight as she passed when every step she took was a seduction? When her dresses squeezed her breasts in front and limned the furrow in her bottom in back? Was it an apricot, he wondered, and then he hated himself for the thought. A peach? A sweet nectarine? Any taste of summer fruit set him wondering, and fruit was something he could not resist. It was hard not to linger outside the bathroom door and breathe the sweet steam that came from her shower until his face was dappled with sweat. It was hard not to want to feel her paling skin with his hands and his mouth. It was hard for things to be the same when they weren't.

At a certain point the shoe man thought, with enormous relief, that her changes had gone as far as they could go. What with beating Robert Smythe by unanimous decision in the second Marilyn Monroe contest she had ever entered, winning fifteen hundred dollars' prize money, the traditional armload of red roses and an opportunity to sign a contract with Resemblances as a Marilyn look-alike model, even Lucille briefly dared to be happy with the current version of her self, until.

Until Buddy said the watery word, nice. Buddy hailed a taxi for the shoe man, who wasn't surprised when Lucille said she'd be home later.

Lucille and Buddy walked nowhere in particular, said nothing much until Buddy drawled, "It's . . . nice. But hardly enough."

"What do you mean nice? It's wonderful. Resemblances wants me. I'm good enough for them and that's good enough for me," Lucille argued, quickening her step and realizing that her feet didn't hurt in her high heels. That was thanks to the shoe man. He appreciated her.

Buddy shrugged. "Then I'm wasting my time," he said, stepping to the curb and raising his arm although there was no cab within blocks of where they stood.

Lucille pulled his arm. He resisted. "Wait. Why?"

"Because they're in it for the money. It's a business. They take a percentage. That's why. Because they do crummy little look-alikes. If that's what you want for yourself, we part here. I don't give a shit about amateur Marilyns and goddamn phony Elvises. Life's too short for waxwork imitations and if that's what you want to be I don't give a shit about you. But it's a goddamn pity, because I do the real thing and you could have been it. Instead, what? You want to be, what? Some imperfect little almost." Buddy spat on the ground. "And they'll let you and they'll tell you that you're good. That's because they don't care about you." A cab stopped beside them. "And I do."

Maybe it was that he said he cared. Who knows? Instead of breaking free on the spot, Lucille wrapped her arms around him until her muscles strained and stood between him and the door handle. "What do you mean could have been?"

She wept as he ripped the Resemblances contract into many more pieces than were necessary to destroy it and let it fall into the black gutter, but she wept silently. "I'll take care of you," he murmured, reaching under her platinum hair to stroke her aching neck. He didn't want to take her to his bed. She wasn't complete.

He drew her down some steps and pressed her back against the gated door of a closed laundromat. His hands mapped her body. He knew it. He knew its flaws. It was his to touch. Feeling the thorns in the bouquet pressed between them and drunk from the sweet rose smell, he could tell her need by her disorderly breathing but he refused to fulfill it. "Let's go, my little Marilyn," he whispered. She shuddered as his breath traced the shell curve of her ear and thought of paradise. She didn't ask where they were going. She didn't really care.

"I wish I was in Hawaii," she said.

"I'll take you to Hawaii," said Buddy. He took her to The Agency. The security guard winked as they passed by, Buddy and the disheveled blonde. He didn't make them sign the register. He knew Buddy. They talked sports. "Somebody's got to get the blondes," he said to himself as he watched Lucille ooze into the elevator.

Buddy unlocked the Hell room and activated the monitor. He poured Lucille a paper cup full of cool water from the dispenser. She put it to her forehead before she sipped. She watched Buddy straddle an upholstered stool as he pressed buttons without watching where his fingers hit. He stared at the screen, forgot her for several minutes, and then Lucille saw her face. In the dark room, on a television screen, it seemed flat, strange, like someone else's face. "That's me," she said.

Buddy ignored her. He brought a grid up over the image and then, with one finger, he fixed it in the computer's memory. With another, he summoned the face of Marilyn Monroe. "Marilyn." The grid reappeared. "Now you." Lucille's face slid on to the screen from left to right. Using the grid, Buddy manipulated her image until it lay directly over Marilyn Monroe's, matching her ears to Marilyn's ears, her nose to Marilyn's nose, her mouth to Marilyn's mouth, her hairline to Marilyn's hairline. When the sandwiching was as exact as it was going to get, Buddy pressed a button and the grid fell out and away leaving a merged face that belonged to neither Marilyn Monroe nor Lucille. "Now watch," said Buddy. He cupped his hand over a grey electronic mouse and moved in across a dull pad. A blue line appeared at the tip of the merged noses. The blue line outlined Marilyn's nose. Buddy pressed a button and those parts of Lucille's nose that did not fall within the blue line were illuminated in red. "Here's the main thing. To start. We'll have to work on the nose."

"How do we work on the nose?" asked Lucille.

"Let's use our little brains. Now how do you *think* we work on the nose?"

Lucille understood. "You want me to get a nose job?"

"You want to be Marilyn?"

"Yeah, but . . ."

"Don't yeah, but, precious."

"I never even had my tonsils out."

"Even Marilyn had to have a nose job to look like Marilyn," Buddy assured her. He put an arm around her shoulder. "And you barely feel it."

"You ever had a nose job?"

Buddy swirled his seat to face her. His eyes were as flat as the eyes on the screen and his voice turned monotone. "Look, we can quit right now."

Lucille nuzzled into his neck. "You don't have to be crabby."

"All right, then," he answered. He showed her where she would need electrolysis to pull her hairline back to create a higher brow. Since she was squeamish, he didn't mention little needles and electric current. "I'll make the appointments. We'll go together." She'd find out. So what? "I'll hold your hand," he said. "The cheeks are good." There was almost no red between her lines and Marilyn's. "The chin is good. And the mouth . . ." Buddy kissed her mouth, holding his lips against her two Marilyn lips, closing his eyes until he pulled away and glanced back at the screen. ". . . is hers. You want to do more?"

"Kisses? Anytime."

"The body."

"No. Kisses."

Buddy obliged. Enough for now.

When he heard her key in the door, the shoe man wrapped

a robe over his T-shirt and shorts and shuffled down the hall to open it. "So." The lipstick had been kissed off her mouth. "A victory celebration?"

"Not exactly," said Lucille. Not unless seeing her imperfections and agreeing to have her nose moved around was a celebration.

"What's wrong?"

"I guess I'm just tired," she said.

The shoe man fixed her a hot cup of camomile tea and sat tenderly beside her as he might have sat beside the child he might have had when the child he might have had came in soaked, shivering and sniffling from the rain. "You did great tonight. No one coulda looked more like Marilyn Monroe except Marilyn Monroe and even she mighta come in second next to you, swear to God."

Lucille began to cry.

"Is it him?"

Lucille shook her head. "No. It's me. I'm not going to sign," she began.

The shoe man didn't understand how, if all she'd wanted was to be a Marilyn model, she had decided—that was how she put it to him, that she herself had decided—not to work for Resemblances.

"I don't want to be just another nobody," she answered.

"Nobody's a nobody," said Jack. "What's a nobody?"

"I don't know," said Lucille.

"Did he call you a nobody? Am I a nobody?" the shoe man persisted. " 'Cause if I am, I'm going to quit paying taxes right here and now."

"You're the most important person in the world," said Lucille, and she kissed him on the forehead. "And I got fifteen hundred casharoony in the bank so tomorrow straight after you close up the shop I'm taking us out to The Steak Place for two filet mignons and baked potatoes."

"And Champagne! On me. To celebrate."

"No, on me."

And so they dickered about who would pay for the Champagne which was a wonderful thing to dicker about, but the important thing is not who bought the brut. The next evening, they ate and drank toasts to each other, to trips to Europe and palm trees in Honolulu and the glorious future ahead and for a few hours there was no Buddy, no thought of a new nose or a higher forehead and Marilyn Monroe was dead and buried, right where she belonged.

ucille's new nose was the most expensive thing she'd ever owned. She'd never had a new car. She'd never owned her own stereo. Now she had a six-thousand-dollar nose, at ninety-five dollars a month plus finance charges. Buddy promised the nose would pay for itself. Within a week the bruises had healed enough to be covered with opaque makeup and the pain could be controlled with a bit of Percodan. She put her nose to work. The tip was numb. She was sure she couldn't smell the muffins that she baked as distinctly as before, but Buddy was right. During that week, Buddy had booked six gigs for the following week. The week after that, she found she'd become opening day queen on the shopping center circuit. Suddenly, she was traveling to upstate New York, New Jersey, Connecticut, Virginia, Maryland, anywhere but Pennsylvania, for a thousand dollars a day plus expenses. Suddenly, she had money in the bank and costumes and bills to pay.

Her act was simple. Lucille, who only used her real name on contracts, would stand on a platform in a white halter dress with a full pleated skirt while passersby watched her skirt blow up to her shoulders. Buddy had rigged the platform so that it had a fan inside. Over the fan was a grate. She wore custom made pantyhose that gave the illusion of bare legs and no panties at all, even going so far as to show a dark triangle at the right place while still obeying decency laws. The only things that were truly bare were her shoulders and arms, and as Buddy liked to say to inquisitive security guards, the Constitution specifically grants us the right to bare arms.

Buddy was her companion on the road, but when she came home, she came home to Jack. The shoe man was delighted. Truth be known, the shoe man was astonished. As soon as he saw her new nose, he thought, That's it. My time is up. He filed down the Lucille angel's nose, enhancing the little bulb at the tip. With some difficulty, he was able to adjust the width, though it meant subtly shaving a layer off the whole front of the face. All the while he worked, he waited for the end, but Lucille showed no signs of leaving for good. When she was away, he found, he rather enjoyed his old solitude. He strode the hall in his torn underwear. He ate Chinese take-out out of the carton. If she was gone more than one night, he waited for the end of that, too. He examined the dresses in what used to be his closet. They were packed so tight together that to pull one from its hanger was to dislodge and rumple three or four on either side. Such dresses. Movie star clothes. Sequins, low necks, lower backs. And she had come to him with one suitcase and a wardrobe of cut-off blue jeans. He remembered her the way she had come into Reliable Repair and the first time she called him Jack, yet already he had forgotten the true color of her eyes. Such changes, so fast. He knew he needed her, even if after he'd had his fresh fruity muffin breakfast he sometimes snuck round to the Haitians for a secret sugary sticky bun or two.

What the shoe man didn't know was that on the road, Lucille had betrayed him.

A multiplex opening had been rained out. She and Buddy took a room at a motel in Schenectady. They were not going to make love. Despite the triumph of her face, she was *still* not Marilyn enough for Buddy to fully desire her and Lucille wasn't one for stopping and starting except when she had to. Buddy kept his awful promise, still refusing her satisfaction for the sake of their shared dream. Her frustration turned to want on her face, and Buddy watched the wanting work its wonders on the faces of the Jims and Bobs and Mikes and

Dicks who turned out to see the hem of her skirt graze her ears. Buddy savored their desire for his little Marilyn and he kept them well away.

But back to the betrayal. It was because there wasn't a lot to do that the conversation began to wander, as it often did these days, in the direction of Jack. Buddy had as little use for Jack as Jack had for him and no use at all for the competition. "What do you need with him?" he demanded to know. "You've got money now."

"I love him." She often answered this way. "And he needs me."

"That's very heartwarming. He needs you. He's an old cock. He probably sniffs your underwear when you're with me."

"Don't be disgusting."

"It's disgusting for a girl like you to live in a place like that with a man like him."

"You don't know what you're talking about."

"I love you."

"I'll tell you what love is," said Lucille. She had been thinking about love since the day the cops came. "Jack. He took me in and didn't lay a finger. He's faithful to his wife. He loves her, even after forty years."

"What wife?"

"He lost her. She disappeared. It broke his heart. And I tried to fix it. I got him a picture of her from the paper. And

I felt so bad. It was all screwed up. It was black where it should have been white and white where it should have been black and it's all he has. You wouldn't understand."

"It's reversed. Five minutes, I could fix it."

"But you couldn't fix his heart." Lucille thought again. "Maybe you could make it really nice?"

"For him?"

"Me. For me." Lucille offered him a wide-mouthed Marilyn smile.

"You're almost perfect," he said.

"If you want to see perfect, that's the other thing. You've got to see his angels. They make Marilyn Monroe look like day-old pizza and worse. I swear."

"Bull," snarled Buddy. "What angels?"

She told him. She told him about heaven in the shoe man's back room, the jewel-eyed angels and the unfinished one who had her face and the police and the murder and how she saved the shoe man from the cops. "Tell me more about the angels," he said. And though they were indescribable, she did the best she could. "And he made them? Where'd he get the gold and the diamonds and shit? How do you know he made them?"

"I know he did. It's hard to believe. They're like . . . They're like . . . They're like God came down and made them himself." Lucille intoned. "Like a miracle."

The awe in her voice enraged him. He'd created her, made

her Marilyn enough to get a thousand clams a day, but did he get awe? No. "I'll show you a miracle. Just wait till I'm finished with you and we'll talk miracles."

"I know," said Lucille. "But Jack is different."

"Bull," he said. He pulled the pilled blanket over his shoulders and head and was silent the rest of the long night. He tried not to think about what Lucille had said and more particularly, the way she had said it, the awe, but it bothered him. It bothered him like an itch in the middle of his back when he was holding groceries in both hands. Nothing could rub it away. He knew the only cure was to see for himself.

What the shoe man didn't know was that not long after they'd returned from Schenectady, Buddy called on Lucille while he was at Reliable Repair. "Happen to be in the neighborhood," he said. He'd never been to visit Lucille. She'd never invited him home and he'd never wanted to come. He didn't believe in Brooklyn. It was off to the side. It was a place that people were from and left as soon as possible. It was not a place to go. He grinned as he looked down the darkened hallway. "If this is your idea of heaven, I got some oceanfront property in Arizona." He ducked and wiped his hand across his forehead. "Whoa! I was nearly hit by a low-flying angel." He pressed his back against the wall. "Get down! Here comes another one."

Lucille wiped her hands on her cutoffs. "You're not funny."

"I dragged my ass out to Brooklyn to see these famous angels and I don't see any angels unless maybe I'm blind."

"They're not here. They're in the back." She led Buddy to the red-topped table and pulled out a chair for him. "And I'm not going to show them to you," she said, but she knew that she would. The secret, their beauty, was too great not to share. She swore him to secrecy, just as she had been sworn. He took the oath. Assuring herself that the shoe man need never know, she opened the back room door.

Rather than feeling relief, Buddy felt his heart clench in his chest and he wanted to vomit. He grabbed his ribs. Everything Lucille had told him was true. Surrounded by the shoe man's angels, Buddy knew someday he'd be dust gone and forgotten, no matter what he did, who he created. We all know that. He knew it worse. His life was nothing, unless . . . His work was nothing, unless . . . These sacred creatures with their wooden mouths and their utter magnificence would outsmile and outscowl and outlive him, unless . . . Transcendent beauty, eternal beauty, made by a man's hand. Not his hand. The shoe man's hand. What right did the shoe man—a nobody, worth nothing, unworthy—have to these angels? No right. What right to the immortality they would bring? No right at all. It was all wrong, unless . . . Unless, yes, the shoe man's hands were merely the road between the angels and their destiny. Yes, it fit perfectly.

Lucille was the key. He was meant to meet her and make

her truly Marilyn but that was just a part. He saw that now.
She, in return, was meant not only to be his temple of
temptation, his masterpiece, but to bring him the gift of
heaven itself if he proved worthy. It was Marilyn's will, her
gratitude for his devotion, that had brought him here
through the body of Lucille. And if he needed proof there
was proof in the angel whose face was a paean to Buddy's
masterful transformation. Did she not have every aspect he
himself had brought to her? Was she not a tender reminder
of the work yet to be done? She was his by right, his and only
his. His and not the shoe man's. And as she presided over the
angels, he was meant to preside, king to her queen, guardian,
master. She needed him. They needed him. They were nowhere and nothing until now. And they would be nothing
without him, helpless darlings, helpless objects that they
were. They were his to cherish or cheapen, to elevate or mar
or burn, even burn, if burning was his will. And they would
make him famous. The world would know his name for he
was truly their creator. The shoe man was a vehicle, a tool,
that was all. Surely he must know the angels were meant for
more than he could give them. What could be more plain?

"Who else has seen these?" he wheezed.

"No one. Only the cops."

"Let's keep it that way." Buddy stood in the room, his
eyes wide, forgetting to breathe, unable to blink, until the
angels began to double and move before his eyes.

He recovered at the red-topped table over one of the shoe man's Budweisers. "Unbelievable." He still whispered, though he was no longer in their presence.

"Yeah, that's the word for it." Buddy ran his finger around and around and around and around the rim of his brown beer bottle until it moaned a sad heavenly moan. Lucille watched his face, afraid to speak until, at last, the hour demanded that she say something. "He'll be coming back," she began. "Unless . . ." She hesitated, hoping he wouldn't want to stay for dinner.

The shock of the angels had subsided, but only slightly. "Right. I better go."

"Could you . . . I mean, since you're here . . ." She held out all that was left of Jack's Angela. "Remember I said about his wife?"

He rolled and unrolled the picture. Another gift. "Bless you, my little Marilyn," he said, trailing his finger across Lucille's white brow and down her left cheek to the penciled mole halfway between her new nose and her reddened lips. He rubbed the mole off with his fingers. No substitutes. Only the real thing would do. "I'll make her better than she ever was, my little goddess, don't you worry."

Surrounded by swerving cars and angry pedestrians, by the urine perfume of subway tunnels, by filthy puddles, blowing newsprint and visible crime, Buddy reveled in the ceaseless tumult of his planning mind. He knew exactly what to do and though he'd called in sick he headed for The Agency.

Ugliness is common. Sores, illness, poverty, dirt, anyone can have and many do. And death. Where's the beauty there, until the skin has fallen away and left the whiteness of the bones? Buddy understood beauty, but probably not quite the way you do. To him, beauty was power. It had to be leashed. Control of beauty was control of life, a bulwark against feeble mortality. Buddy was not moved by the tragedy of Marilyn Monroe. He found her weakness pathetic. He was moved by her desirability as he was moved to re-create it, no *create* it, in Lucille. And it was something like that with the angels. They didn't touch his soul nor move him, even for an instant, to a height above himself and his own aspirations. They challenged him. And he had to win or lose all. And so, Buddy schemed. In his head he made a list of what needed to be done. He didn't write it down. Only a fool would have written it down and provided the world with clear evidence.

Meanwhile, Lucille strived to please. Without being aware of how it happened, she came to feel she was never more herself than when she was regarded as Marilyn. Alone, when she might once have been at ease, she was now unsure of what to do. She needed to be watched. She didn't know how she'd ever felt otherwise and she told Buddy so, and he said, "Good, good. We're getting somewhere." It bothered her that the shoe man worked alone. She begged the shoe man to let her model for her angel. *Her* angel.

He didn't say no. He just changed the subject. At night, when Lucille was asleep, or on the weekends, when she was apt to be opening a Marshall's somewhere, the shoe man carefully worked his way down the Lucille angel's body, past her shoulders, to her breasts and worked around them out of a modesty so deep he could not displace it. There would be time, he told himself, for the pleasure of shaping her bosom, but even alone in his room in the dark he could not lay his hands over the rough wooden hemispheres without a certain unease. He carved the gentle waves of skin that rolled over her ribs and the typical slightly lopsided tilt of her hips. Then he reached her bottom, and again, shyness hindered his progress. This was Lucille's bottom and those were Lucille's breasts. He had no doubt he could carve them to within a quiver of life, sand them so soft that the wood would seem to yield under his fingers, but his hands refused their assignment.

He tried to ignore his frustration. Turning away from her breasts and her bottom, he carved a fine summer down on her forearms. He replaned the slope of her shoulders. Gave her collarbone a ballerina's definitions and slightly reshaped the middle bones of her spine so that the wings he had yet to carve would seem to grow naturally from the center of her back. But he could not finish her legs, nor could he perfect her belly until he did what he had to do. Despair began to slow his walk, dulling even the tingle he enjoyed every night as he swallowed his pungent, cold beer. There was no ignoring the truth. His beloved Lucille angel was a curse. He knew she might also be the finest angel he would ever carve, if only . . .

He wondered when Lucille might again offer her body to his eyes. Maybe that's what the angel demanded of him. Maybe that was her message, her taunt, her test. He just might say yes, he thought to himself. Damn Angela. It was all her fault. If he'd been loving her every night for the past forty years, none of this would be happening. Where had she been? Where was she now? What the hell? He just might. What the hell? He might not. He wasn't going to ask her outright. He couldn't. What if Lucille peeled away her clothes on the spot? What would happen then? After forty years without a real woman in his arms? What?

Though Lucille detected a change and feared its meaning, none of his customers paid any attention to the shoe man's distracted mid-sentence pauses. If they figured anything at all, they figured he was getting old. And Gloria the pizza lady figured he was being eaten up by guilt. Those were her exact words. Eaten up by guilt. She wondered why he hadn't been arrested and blamed the city budget cuts for letting criminals walk free. But never mind about her.

One day, not very long after he'd seen the angels, Buddy walked through the jingling door of Reliable Repair carrying a chamois cloth shoe bag. "How ya doin', Jack?" he said as he pulled out a pair of black cowboy boots. The shoe man saw at once that the squared toes had gone ragged with scuffing. The black hide peeled back on itself where ankle rubbed against ankle. The heels were worn down on the inside instead of the usual place.

"These are very fine boots," said the shoe man as he analyzed Buddy's strange stance. Maybe his weight distribution was skewed by the heavy cameras hanging over his neck. "Crocodile."

"Very expensive and very endangered." Buddy grinned. If the shoe man had been of a different mind, he might have been suspicious not only of the grin but of the visit. Surely there were shoe repair men wherever Buddy lived. "Marilyn says you're the best around."

"I am." The shoe man wasn't flattered by a plain fact. Certainly not when it came from the lips of Buddy Lomax. "You mean Lucille. It'll cost you a lot." The shoe man picked the highest number he could think of. "It'll cost you, I'd say, two hundred bucks to make these right." The shoe man thought that would get rid of him.

It didn't. "Whatever."

Leaning into his work lamp, the shoe man rubbed his thumb across the irregular texture of the crocodile hide. "The animal was too young."

"Listen, what if I told you I could make your dreams come true?"

"You can pull that on her but not on me."

"Who's pulling?" Buddy slid a photograph out of his pocket and placed it face up in the shoe man's hand.

It was Angela at the height of her beauty. Angela with a slight peachy blush narrowing toward the bridge of her nose. Angela with her wine-colored lips partway open and Angela with her sea storm eyes and Angela with her freckled upper arm and Angela with a trace of rounded breast under her lace-trimmed blouse. He didn't remember the blouse, but it had to be her. It had to be her blouse because she was wearing it. "How did you . . ." It was a color picture. How could that be? He and Angela had never had a color camera. Were there color cameras forty years ago? What difference did it make? It had to be her. There was no doubt in the shoe man's mind. What the shoe man didn't know was that it was and wasn't Angela. It was a composite, created in the Hell. It was Angela based on what the shoe man had told Lucille and what Lucille had told Buddy and what Buddy had patched together from the wedding photo and the paintbox function and an early publicity shot of Sophia Loren. The shoe man's eyes would not leave the photograph. If it was a hallucination, he did not want it to end. "Angela," he whispered.

Buddy placed a second picture on the shoe man's bench. A woman of no particular age. Older, that was all. The kind of woman who became more beautiful as life added its layers to her face. Tanned. Slender. Smiling, not too broadly. Smiling as if she knew what others had yet to learn. Her hair was the pale shade of blonde that women over fifty tend to wash over their grey. But she had Angela's eyes, outlined by a spider web. And Angela's lips, painted too red. And where do you suppose this picture came from? "This is her now," was all he said.

The shoe man forced himself to look. "It isn't possible." He placed the two pictures edge to edge and saw they were the same woman. No doubt. There was no doubt. "How . . . Where is she?" he whispered frantically. "Did she give you these? Where the hell is she?" He was shouting now. "What did she say, goddamnit?" He squeezed Buddy's arm so tight he stopped the blood. "Where is she? What did she say?"

"I don't know."

"Tell me."

Buddy chuckled. "I said I don't know."

The shoe man clenched his eyes against the laughter and as the snaking crimson veins thrashed in protest, he prayed to God his spasming, boiling, spitting heart would stop now, forever. In the red-streaked darkness, he waited to die. His wish was not heard. If heard, it was not granted. He smelled a hellish sulphur. A match. Buddy lit a cigarette. He sucked. He puffed. He blew smoke in the air. A white flash penetrated his shut eyes and the shoe man flinched. Buddy had taken a picture. A photograph of his private agony. What right? What right? The shoe man considered murder. All he needed was before him here in Reliable Repair. Knives. Needles. Hammers. Well-sharpened shears. But if he rid himself of Buddy, what of Angela? Why had she come to him now through this monster? His Angela needed him at last. At last she needed him and he could not fail her. "What do you want?"

Buddy pretended to consider the question. At last, he answered. "The angels," he said. "The angels are mine."

The shoe man no longer knew if his eyes were open or

closed. What did it matter? Everything was black. "Out," he growled. And he heard a stranger say the word. His voice belonged to a man whose thundering pain was so explosive that there was no release, and trapped, rumbling through his muscles again and again, it collapsed in upon him. The doorbells jingled and the frame slammed shut. The shoe man willed himself to see. Buddy had disappeared, leaving the boots and the pictures behind. Though it was early in the day, the shoe man locked his shop and left it. He could not bear to remain there. He could not bear to go home. He stared up at stuffed Angie in the window and offered God a second chance to take him. God did not oblige. Not exactly. But the man the shoe man had been was gone.

The shoe man walked spirals in the park, around the perimeter and in and in toward the great center lawn. Carelessly aware of the danger, he walked behind isolated thickets and under shadowy bridges, but no one attacked him, no one even begged a quarter from his pocket. No gunshots echoed through the dale. No foam-mouthed mongrel skewered him with its fangs. No sirens deafened him to all thought. He walked in peace without distraction, his misery undisturbed. No matter how he angled his thoughts, they returned to the same sad fact. Lucille had betrayed his secrets.

That she had come to him was his fate. That she had betrayed him, what was that?

His sorrow rode his shoulders, wrapping around his arms like a thick and heavy python. When a breeze whisked the sweat from his face, a brisk anger would singe his cheeks, but it would pass, whereas the sorrow only got heavier and heavier and heavier as he carried it with him.

He knew Lucille. He thought he knew Lucille. She loved him. He dared believe she loved him, in some way, like a father or an uncle or the carver of her angel. So. Why? There was no reason. There had to be a reason. Whatever it was, Lucille's betrayal could not be washed away with berry muffins and fresh perked, even her berry muffins and her fresh perked. He knew he ought to banish her from his life for what she'd done, but whose loss, whose punishment, was that?

Darting down Vanderpole toward Parker like a butterfly dodging a net, he made his way home. But it wasn't home anymore. He was afraid to enter the hallway. He was afraid to place his key in the lock. He was afraid to open the door. He was afraid everything would be altered. He was afraid everything would seem the same. He was afraid to see her. What in heaven's name was he supposed to say? And then it occurred to him. Perhaps, he thought, perhaps his mind had wandered to the edge of a ravine and his pain was just an old man's folly. Perhaps the sight of his sweet Lucille would make a lie of his torture.

She bounded to the door at the sound of the turning knob. "Guess what!" she sang.

"What?"

"Buddy got me a commercial 'cause he works for The Agency and he has contacts, you know, in the business and it's national but I can't say what yet 'cause I really don't know or I'd tell you first of anyone and it's a ton of money to start and then royalties so I get money all the time and I can afford my new boobs and who knows what-all else and you and me can . . ." She stopped. Jack's head hung between his hunched shoulders like a shriveled apple clinging in death to a snow heavy branch. She knew. "Oh, Jack." She held his sad head to her breast and stroked it. He hadn't the strength to pull away. "How?"

"He has Angela."

"He can't. I'd know if he did."

"He has pictures. He came to the shop." All he had to say was "out," but whose loss, whose punishment, was that? His tears wet her blouse as he thought of the lonely consequences. No more sweet-scented steam on the mirror. No one to call him Jack. "He wants the angels."

"The picture is a fake. It's all my fault. He has a machine. It . . ."

"It's as real as she was, is."

Lucille explained about the angels and the sorry wedding photo. "I was so proud of you and I thought . . ."

"You were so proud?" His knees fell out beneath him. Lucille caught him. "Oh, God, oh, Jesus." The shoe man began to pant. Each breath released a little cry. Lucille slid his back down the wall to the floor and propped him there as she ran for water.

She bathed his face, his neck, his chest with her fingers. "That bastard. I told him never . . ." Buddy had broken the same promise she had broken and with less cause to keep it. "I'll kill him . . . I'll never speak to that . . ."

The shoe man struggled to force the words through his throat. "You don't get it. He has her picture from now. She's somewhere."

"If she's somewhere, well, why wouldn't she just, you know, come home, I mean?"

"There are hundreds of reasons." The shoe man tested three or four. In trouble. In debt. Illness. She would have to know he'd help her even now. It didn't make sense. Maybe she'd been deceived. Maybe she didn't even know he was alive. "Maybe he's holding her hostage. I wouldn't put it past. How the hell should I know what the hell is . . ." His heart beat out of rhythm and he put his hand to his chest. "Ah, Lucille, Lucille, what you do to me. Sometimes I think you'll be the death, I have to say."

"Do you want me to . . ." Lucille joined the shoe man in a wish to stop all time. "Maybe you want me to go?"

"No." She was too dear to him.

Lucille kissed his forehead. "We'll get her back, don't worry."

"I can't think."

"Me neither." Lucille helped the shoe man to his bed that was now her bed. She tucked him under a flowered cotton sheet, stroking his face as if her touch would cauterize the wounds she had inflicted. "You'll stay with me." She knew what to do when life made living unbearable. "You're my sweetheart. Let's watch TV," she said. And she crawled under the sheet beside him.

The only lust the shoe man felt was the lust for an ancient memory that returned to him that night. He remembered how it was to be enveloped in his mother's arms, the warm spicy smell, the loose soft skin. If only he could have stayed there forever, he thought. There was always comfort there, and surety. Lucille held him now, and he let her. She stroked the wiry hair upon his head and rocked him slightly, saying, "Shhh shhh shhh, Mama's here." How did she know what to say? She didn't know. She just did what she felt to be right, and for once, it was.

In the morning, she was out of bed before Jack woke from his dream. She didn't want to answer the questions that would come with his waking with her beside him though she knew Jack wouldn't ask them.

She did what she always did when she had the jitters and her hands needed busying. She tried a new recipe.

The shoe man and Lucille ate their zucchini-walnut muffins in silence. A gulf of caution lay between them. Much as both of them wished, more than wished, the day before had never happened, it had. And it would have been unwise, if not impossible, to say nothing more about it. Something had to be done. Neither knew what that something was. How could they know?

Munching the nuts, listening to the hiss of the percolator, it was understood that neither Jack nor Lucille could bear to live without the other. That didn't need saying. But what about Angela? What about Buddy? Jack had thrown him out, but that wasn't the end. It couldn't be the end if he had to find Angela. Buddy was his bloodhound.

"You might not even . . . You don't even know if . . . I don't know . . . Maybe it's best if you . . ." Lucille arrived at the question. "Could you live without knowing?"

"After I seen her picture? Could you if you was me?"

She didn't know. "I'll do whatever you want," said Lucille. And she meant it. Though Lucille knew she needed Buddy to become who she was meant to be, though she knew that Marilyn was someone she would never be without his molding, she was prepared to say she'd seen her maker for the last time. She was prepared to leave her Marilynization unfinished for Jack's sake. She was prepared. "Maybe . . ."

"If you hadn't seen your wife for forty years . . ."

"And you still loved her," she added.

157

"And you still loved her and there might be some way . . ."

"Oh, Jack, I'm so sorry. I should have never . . . This is all my fault."

"Nah, only half. The rest . . ." The rest was Angela's fault for having left him in the first place. His troubles traced back to that damnable day. He understood now why God kept women out of heaven. God wasn't as dumb as he looked. "What a mess. Could you?"

"No. Maybe."

"Yeah, exactly." The shoe man rubbed his chin against the back of his hand. "We got to deal with this bastard. I don't see how else . . ."

"If you say." An involuntary shiver of relief escaped her body. She despised herself for it. "What about the angels?"

The shoe man inspected his stubble-scratched hand. He flipped his palm out, wiggled his fingers and smiled. "I'd rather set their wings on fire. That fuckin' . . ."

Lucille took his fingers in her hand. "Let me walk you to the shop."

There were twenty-four red roses resting on the welcome mat outside the shoe man's door. The card read, *To Marilyn with undying love. A fan.*

"Well, at least that's nice," said the shoe man.

Every morning until the end the roses came, twenty-four each time, always the same, always red, always with undying love. Until the end.

There's something you ought to know. Buddy didn't really expect the shoe man to say, Sure. Take my angels. Please.

His expulsion from Reliable Repair was no surprise to him. He welcomed the challenge to his art. And it was a challenge. If he met it, he had no doubt he would prevail.

As for Lucille's angry appearance at his apartment, he'd predicted that, too, and as vexing as it was to hear his good name ravaged by a storming woman, he was rather pleased with himself. He stayed overlong on the toilet, paging through *National Geographic* so that Lucille could have all the time she might want to search his desk and drawers for clues of Angela. He knew she would. She was doing him a favor.

He flushed.

Lucille blocked his exit at the bathroom door. "Where is she?" she snarled.

"That's a very unbecoming tone of voice, my little Marilyn."

"I'm not your anything unless you tell me where she is!"

"Darling, I told him. I have no idea."

Lucille waved a Xerox of the aged photograph he had given the shoe man. Jack was unwilling to let his copy leave his sight even for an hour. "What's this?"

"A terrible Xerox of an excellent, probably better than in life, version of the famous lost Angela at approximately fifty-eight years of age, in good health, with moderate drinking habits and a penchant for golf, which is what I figure women who look like her do."

"So you made her up?"

"On my sweet little Hell."

"I hate you for this."

"You can't afford to hate me, little Marilyn. And besides . . ." Buddy tousled Lucille's Champagne hair, noting that the roots were a little muddy. "I'm only trying to help." He kissed her cheek. "Your skin could be baby soft with a little dermabrasion. It doesn't hurt. They freeze your face. Maybe a little sting. That's all. And presto. Porcelain white."

"No."

"Well, we'll think about it later."

"I want you to come with me to Jack and apologize for making the whole thing up."

"Don't be an idiot. People pay good money for pictures like that. I'm giving him a chance to locate her."

"Great. What's he supposed to hire a detective? He doesn't have money for that."

"If he sells his angels . . ."

"He'd rather die."

Buddy shrugged. "If you say so," he said. And then he hummed an annoying tune as he changed his clothes and slid into a raincoat. "I'm going out. You can stay here if you want."

"Stay away from him."

"If you say so."

"I'll pay for it. Whatever it costs."

"I see," said Buddy. He took her elbow and led her down the hall, past the doorman, out into the rain. "A beautiful little girl is going to have to work very, very hard to pay for all the things she has to pay for, isn't she?" Buddy placed his two hands over Lucille's breasts. "We're going to be so happy with these fixed." He slid his hands down her ribs to her waist. "And this is a little present from your Buddy who loves you." He pressed her hips against his so she could feel what she'd done to him.

His hardness aroused her, not only because his desire was

so exacting and she had waited for it, but because of a hot spark of hate for him and herself. She closed her eyes and pictured herself strangling Buddy with a kiss, kissing him until he twitched and spasmed and struggled and died. She rested her hands on his shoulders. It wouldn't be so hard to drive a knife between his shoulder blades if she had a knife, but she didn't. She trembled. She always trembled when he touched her. It wasn't something she could help.

"I want you, Marilyn," he whispered, but that was the end of it.

t was late, too late to replace the bulb over the red-topped table. Her face was white with fatigue, and the way her mascara had smudged her eyes into shadow, she looked like a skull in a tight short-sleeved sweater. The shoe man wondered if Lucille had cracked. She was trying to explain the Hell and how it worked. Jack wasn't having any and she didn't blame him. "But it's true," she whined.

"He's got you hoodwinked within an inch," Jack argued. "Because what you're telling me isn't painting out the wrinkles on Elizabeth Taylor's face. Which, by the way, is no secret that they do, according to Gloria at the pizzeria who knows the sister of the woman who dyes her hair which, by the way, isn't naturally black anymore. If what you're tell-

ing me . . . then everything goes out the window. Kaplooey.
You're saying when those spaceships go up, maybe they're
just going round the block and someone's making up pictures of the universe? That's what you're saying. And that's
a completely different thing."

"Did you see us go to the moon?" Lucille retorted. "How
do you know?" Buddy made her doubt everything.

"That's the whole point of a photograph. So you don't
have to be there to know the facts. Or else how would you
know what happened? If what you're saying, it would be so
easy to fudge that pictures would be useless. You could fake
anything and who's to know? They could show things that
never happened and say they did and vicey versey and
meanwhile I'm getting one hell of a headache."

"Me too," said Lucille.

"So we agree on something," said Jack.

Lucille laughed. "I want to see my angel."

The arrow sharp sorrow he felt at even the thought of his
beloved angels was so deep that the shoe man avoided enter-
ing his back room unless he was so exhausted he could
pretend they weren't there as he waited for sleep to save
him. His intolerable distress stretched out of mind sight.
Like a medieval map of the unseen seas, it teemed with
monsters and sucked him toward the uncharted edge that
divided life from nothingness. When he had to think about
his angels at all, the shoe man found a simple explanation for

his new aversion to them. He told himself that since he could not convince Lucille to abandon her plans to reshape and resize her breasts in favor of a more sensible investment like a car or an Individual Retirement Account, he was waiting until her new shape was determined to do the breasts on his Lucille angel. And that is what he told Lucille.

Meanwhile, Buddy hired a detective. Of his own choosing, as you've no doubt surmised. He gave the detective the aged version of the shoe man's Angela without saying where it came from. Buddy told him what little he knew of the long-lost woman and said, "Find her."

"Last name?"

"It's probably changed."

The detective said, "You haven't given me a lot to go on. Is there a missing persons?"

"Doubt it, at this point."

"Well, the first thing I'd do is circulate this here picture around to the police."

"No police. No milk cartons. No cereal boxes. Just find her," said Buddy. "And if you can't find her, find her anyway."

The detective understood even if you do not. And, on the morning she was to star in her now famous Big Bob's Root Beer commercial, Buddy told Lucille that everything was now under control. That made her almost happy. The part of her that wasn't happy altered her well-known Marilyn smile, adding a heart-wrenching winsomeness that caused the members of the camera crew to shudder in awe. The camera loved it. Cameras love pain. Lucille stood as she always stood. Over a grate in a white silk halter dress. She held her dress down in front just as Marilyn had. Then a man, faceless, so that every man in America could picture himself in his place, handed her a bottle of Big Bob's Root Beer. As she took it, she released her skirt, and it blew up past her ears in the usual way, only this time her panties read "Drink Big Bob's." And she was asked to say, "So cool it's hot. Ooh!" Lucille said these stupid words as if they meant something, just as the late Marilyn would have done. She imbued them with all the sexual pleasure she'd been denied and more. Remnants of hurt and confusion slipped into her whisper. She couldn't help it. She offered to say the words over again, but the director was happy. "What a performance!" he shouted.

The client was ecstatic. The Agency executives murmured among themselves about all the awards they would win, and there was some talk among upper management of taking Buddy off the Hell and moving him into Creative. Buddy put an end to the talk as soon as he heard it and accepted a raise instead.

The Agency paid Lucille promptly. As soon as the check was deposited in the bank, Lucille settled into her room at the Harbinger Clinic. Her nose job had been an in and out

procedure. Dermabrasion was another quickie. In in the
A.M., sandpaper the face, and out, pink, polished and in pain
by lunch, the latest. Even reshaping two breasts to Marilyn
Monroe's generously airborne contours was a one-day procedure with two days of bedrest, but. The but was the ribs.
First of all, cosmetic surgeons just plain didn't *do* ribs and
second, even if they did, she'd be confined for several weeks
and restricted for weeks after that. "I can't," said Lucille.
She told Buddy to forget about the ribs.

He told her there was nothing worse than a quitter. She'd
have the nose, the breasts, the skin to add to the hair, the
smile, the walk and the whisper, the wanting and the very
soul, but she'd never be Marilyn without some work on the
waist. Nature had cheated her out of her due. Made her thick
where, by Marilyn's sacred memory, she ought to have been
thin. And how could her hips ever assume their fullest grace,
their erotic, rolling destiny, if they were topped off by a cut
of salami when they ought to have been the rounded base of
a handblown vase that curved to touch the stem of the rose
within it? How could she come so far and then settle for
inexactitude when she was two ribs away from her deepest
desire, and his? Buddy had already located a Hollywood
specialist who was willing to remove the lowest rib on each
side and reshape the rib above it, in conjunction with a
plastic surgeon who would tighten her waistline from the
inside out, leaving only a hairline scar in the same exact

location that Marilyn Monroe had had a scar from her appendix operation.

"You'll be perfection."

Lucille knew he was right. There was so little Lucille left, she might as well get rid of it all. "My own mother wouldn't recognize me!"

"As soon as you're yourself, we'll check into the Plaza. You and me. Buddy Lomax and Marilyn Monroe in the best suite money can buy. And we won't leave the room for two days. Three. Four. We'll live on oysters . . ."

"And Champagne . . ." Lucille could see her life beginning new. She would be Marilyn. Buddy would love her one hundred percent. She'd be rich. Jack would have Angela. And everything, everything would be perfect. "And then we'll hold a press conference!"

Picturing her triumph, she forgot about the angels. Buddy never forgot about the angels. They were his last thought at night and his first thought in the morning.

Lucille wanted to discuss what they would tell the press, but she sensed that Buddy wasn't with her anymore. He was smiling, but his smile had set and stiffened. He wasn't looking at her. He wasn't looking at anything she could see. "Come back," she said. "You scared me."

"I'm just thinking," Buddy answered. "You're my masterpiece." The pink walls of her Harbinger suite flattered her skin, and even in her seersucker robe and terry slippers, she was magnificent. After the surgery, she would be sublime and his work would be done and he would be the man, the only man, who possessed the new and only Marilyn Monroe. Body and soul. What then? What next?

BUDDY PLANS
FOR THE FUTURE

ther men had seen photographs of Marilyn Monroe and sighed about being born too late, as if time were the only thing that obstructed their union with the world's most famous sex symbol since Helen of Troy. Some had obsessed and written books. Many contented themselves with sticky dreams.

They didn't make women like that anymore. *They* didn't. Buddy did. Buddy was the one who challenged time. Buddy was the one who outwitted history. No, he wasn't the richest or the handsomest or the smartest man alive, but he was the one who would, in a matter of weeks, share a bed with the incomparable Marilyn, tailor made, just for him.

So what was the problem?

Ah. What is always the problem as one anticipates the culmination of one's most highly cherished lifelong fantasy? The morning after. And though the morning after was yet to come, Buddy, who was always thinking ahead, could already feel it.

He didn't let himself sink. He repaired to Grand Central Terminal with his camera and spent the morning hours photographing hairstyles, hairlines, eyes, eyebrows, noses, lips, chins, jaws, cheeks, necks, ears, fingers, wrists, forearms and upper arms, elbows, buttocks, hips, knees, thighs, calves, shoes, breasts, torsos and lots and lots of children's faces to transfer to the modified Hell ultra-high-resolution image database that he had boasted about to Lucille.

The transfer was done in a matter of hours. After that, the computer sorted the images, breaking them down by type so that Buddy had a file for each body part at the ready. He called the bridal image of Angela onto the screen and placed his clearest photograph of the shoe man beside it. Angela, as you remember, was nineteen. The shoe man, over sixty. Reducing Angela's image by 87.5 percent, he moved it to the upper right hand corner of the screen and magnified Jack as he dissolved his face into thousands of color-graded pixels. First Buddy worked the edges, tightening Jack's jaw, eliminating the weight of age from his cheeks and neck, youthening the earlobes, and removing overall wrinkles and the troutish mottling that covered the shoe man's healthy brown hide. With sixteen million possible colors and two hundred and fifty greys, Buddy could shade the shoe man's face to show the work he'd done in the morning and whether he'd had an argument or made love the night before.

Working inside the perimeters of a twenty-year-old man's face, Buddy unaged the eyes, slimmed the nose and removed the pitting from the bridge. On a hunch, he shrank the mole on his chin, dabbing it away with the light pen. Even if the mole had been there in his youth, the shoe man would recall it as less prominent. Buddy understood vanity, and in working backward, he had the option of showing the shoe man's youthful handsomeness to the best possible advantage. The mouth required the most delicate work. Eyes can easily be brightened, but sadness takes root in the mouth. Buddy filled out the lips and reddened them, but he could not rid them of their melancholia. He wondered if it had always been there, if it had had something to do with Angela's disappearance. It took several hours to manipulate the mouth, pixel by pixel, until the composite smile on the shoe man's adapted face was that of a lucky man. Buddy filled in the hair, making it thick and wavy, just the way a man wants to remember his hair when he is old and it is mostly gone. Then he duplicated and filed the shoe man's altered face as a basis for future work.

He returned Angela to half screen and dissolved the boundaries between her image and Jack's. It was easy to render a history for the young couple, really just a matter of transplanting heads onto other images from the period and adjusting the shadows, time on the clock, perspective and color gradation to eliminate any evidence of a fabricated image. He created a pregnant Angela. An Angela in the hospital, babe in arms. The shoe man with a cigar in his mouth. The new family on the stoop of the Parker Street apartment building. But then Buddy had to decide how many children the shoe man and Angela might have had. He settled on one. Somehow one child seemed more poignant when you considered the loss. And knowing how the shoe man felt about Lucille, Buddy made it a girl and gave her the features of the young Marilyn Monroe, whose childhood pictures were plentiful. Buddy altered the well-known images so that they could not be placed, carefully reflecting the coloration and features of her might-have-been parents. He put her in a kiddie pool. On a swing at the park. With the shoe man and Angela beside her as she rode a game farm pony. Hand in hand with Jack on the first day of kindergarten. In a white communion dress, looking like an angel.

And when Buddy had falsified a most plausible, better than plausible, an *ideal* family history, untaxed by quarrels, mishap or grief, he transferred the digital images to negatives. Some were black and white. Most were color. Though it pained him, he degraded the purity of the tones for the sake of authenticity. They couldn't appear to be magazine quality. They had to look more real than life itself, which in this case meant somewhat scruffy. He took the negatives to a variety store toward the end of the Number 7 line in Queens. It was owned by a Bengali man whose wife suffered from glaucoma. He was too cheap to hire another employee, so it was she who did the job. Not only was the wife notoriously bad at photo processing, her husband could be relied upon to use expired chemicals and the lowest quality paper.

The results were better than even Buddy had hoped. Next, he baked the photographs on a low heat. Some cooked for five minutes, some for fifteen, depending on how old they were supposed to be. He poured water on one series, froze the pictures, then defrosted them. The rest he spread across his kitchen counter to be smudged with butter, scratched by toast, circled with coffee stains and eroded by detergent just as well-loved, often admired family pictures should be.

If he had been anything less than a perfectionist, he might have considered the job done. But, no. There would be no family album without an album. Finding an unused one that might have been bought by a shoe man or his pretty wife in or about 1950 wasn't a project for a man of weak resolve. Buddy rented a van and shopped every garage sale in and around Buffalo, New York, for two weekends in a row. Why Buffalo? Because that is the sort of thing one finds in Buffalo. And Buddy found it. In embossed maroon leather for eight dollars.

s for Lucille, who knew nothing of the album, Buddy phoned her several times a day to say he loved her. He sent a life-size stuffed panda. He sent chocolate cream–filled truffles flown fresh from Brussels. He did everything but visit, and she understood. He didn't want to see her until she was wholly Marilyn, and she passed hours in the day imagining Buddy's eyes, tears at the corners unmasking his helpless desire, as he beheld her perfection. Sometimes she continued the fantasy between pink satin sheets. If she thought about Jack and how Buddy had hurt him, she pictured Marilyn spurning his love, laughing at his nakedness, stalking away on the arm of, say, Elvis Presley, only someone alive, and virile, who would want her and want her and always want her.

The shoe man avoided thinking about Buddy at the same time he thought about Lucille. He didn't like where those thoughts led. He was glad they didn't meet at the hospital. Glad, and a bit baffled.

The shoe man visited Lucille faithfully each evening after he locked up Reliable Repair, bringing a carton of sweet and sour pork to share for supper. He sat by her bedside and fed her with a sterling fork provided by the clinic.

Each evening, he emptied the glass vase on her nightstand and replaced yesterday's red roses with the identical new batch that had come addressed with a fan's undying love. And they joked about it. He did most of the laughing. She couldn't. He would have done anything to take away her pain. He had opposed her surgery, he was repulsed by the results. He understood that in the end, after all the healing, she would be beautiful, but to him, she had been beautiful before her first alteration. He wanted to ask her why all this was necessary, but he didn't. He thought the question cruel under the circumstances. Besides, it was too late.

Her face had been scraped to a brilliant pink; her eyes were ringed with Vaseline. She could not bear to wear her contact lenses. Bloody tributaries meandered away from her foggy pupils. The shoe man winced at her bandaged ribs each time he saw her work to breathe, but she swore they barely hurt her. Resting her hands around her neck because her breasts were too tender to tolerate even the weight of her own fingers, she would whisper, "Thank heaven for morphine." When her eyes closed, her face relaxed and he kissed the ends of her hair, which was already dead and couldn't hurt, and then he would take the subway home alone.

The shoe man discovered that being alone for weeks was different from being alone for weekends, time to time, and that being alone for weeks was in many ways more difficult than being alone for years.

It wasn't as if Lucille had gone from Friday to Sunday to open a shopping center in McLean and he could lounge happily in a dirty shirt eating the muffins she'd left for him while awaiting her return.

And it wasn't as if she had left him for the bright lights and he could grow accustomed to the loss, which was something he, sadly, knew well how to do.

It was right in between. She was away for a matter of weeks. And it was hard. He reminded himself he could count backward to her return, but he forgot to eat breakfast. He told himself it was a good time to catch up with old friends, but Gloria the pizza lady pretended not to know what he wanted when he showed up for lunch and ordered the usual. And at night after he ate Chinese with Lucille at the clinic and took the train home alone, he didn't quite know where to sleep.

If he slept on the couch, as he had done for almost a year—a year!—he slept with the angels. *If* he slept. What had come to him so naturally, as naturally as the leaves came to the oak next door, was now a struggle. In the company of his angels, he could not help but search for the moment he had gone wrong. Was it when he had visited Leopoldine? Was it when Lucille appeared? Was it the dream of a lady angel that had misled him? Or was he in a fix because his lips missed Angela's on the day she disappeared down the subway steps?

If he slept in his own bed he dreamt of Lucille's breasts, Angela's lips and no faults but his own manly weakness, his own stumped desires. Sometimes Lucille visited him and kissed the musty places he touched only for utilitarian reasons. Sometimes Angela stormed into the room, admonishing him for his infidelity. Sometimes she brought him back to their earliest nights together, whispering her secret words in his ear and lifting him higher than mere heaven. Sometimes he was at a funeral.

He woke unrested.

Wherever he chose to spend the night, he felt the consequences in the morning. He was tired as he worked at his bench. He squinted as the sun shattered across the dusty window, blinding him to the view, sealing him in his loneliness. If the people passing his window looked in his direction, which they were not likely to do, they saw the shoe man talking to himself. He wasn't talking to himself. He was discussing his dilemma with stiff, dusty Angie, the glass-eyed parrot who had died but never deserted him, and on her silent advice, he chose his dreams over the angels and waited for a sign.

There were several.

On that day he had two meaningful visits. The first was from Officers Ullman and Couch. Oh, they entered smiling and asked after the shoe repair business and Lucille Bixby's long since healed scraped knee, her resemblance to Marilyn Monroe and her modeling career. Couch told him there'd been a racial squabble in front of headquarters and TV cameras had been there to make sure it made the news. The shoe man felt relaxed enough to shrug. "A squabble is nothin'. It's a miracle we don't have war," he said. He'd once counted twelve languages spoken in the neighborhood: Russian, Albanian, Arabic, Hindi, Japanese, Spanish, Korean, Chinese, French, Creole, Italian and English English, not to mention American, which made thirteen. "You got a pernt," said Couch. Ullman complained about the unbreathing polyester in his uniform causing a rash where his arm holster rubbed and asked if the shoe man knew what to do for corns. And so on. After ten, fifteen minutes of convivial chat, Ullman looked at his watch and said, "Nice to see ya." And the shoe man said, "Likewise."

The door slammed. The bells tinkled. Officers Ullman and Couch left the shop without a word about the mass murderer or their investigation into his death. The shoe man considered that a good sign.

How was he to know?

The shoe man made no mistake about the second sign. A visit from Buddy Lomax was never good. Without a greeting, the shoe man fetched Buddy's black boots from the back of the store and handed him a bill. Buddy admired the work. "Pay and get out," the shoe man answered.

"No reason to be snippy," said Buddy. "I have a present for you."

"I don't want it. Take the boots for free. Just go."

Buddy took the boots and left the maroon leather album with his business card clipped to the cover. The shoe man threw it in the trash.

If only he'd had the strength to dump it along with the daily *Post* and the leather scraps and the Kleenex and the waxed-paper coffee cups into the green plastic bag that he tied tight and winged over the top of the corner Dumpster at the end of the day.

If only he'd resisted one little peek.

If only.

PANDORA'S ALBUM

What would you have done? The album was a magnet. Its pull was more than the shoe man could stand. The first peek led to the turning of one page, and the turning of one led inevitably to the turning of the next. It was his life he saw pictured, the life he should have had with his cherished wife, Angela, who had never disappeared, who had bounded up the subway steps and into Reliable Repair and into his arms carrying paper bags stuffed full of lacy brassieres and petticoats, with the little daughter they conceived during their lunchtime siestas, who had Angela's thick hair and his dark eyes and Angela's laugh and his tenderness and Angela's long legs and his strong hands and so on.

And the moments, the missing moments. The loss of these moments had left him a lifetime scavenger for small particles of happiness, knowing the big joys had evaded him. And there they were, found and whole, evidence he'd suffered sweeping amnesia, that everything had been just fine all along and he'd suddenly recalled his great happiness in family life. But it wasn't that simple. He didn't remember. How could he remember what had never happened? And at the same time, he felt that yes, he did remember, that the life he saw was his life, in black, white and color. Halfway through the album, the pictures stopped. The album was unfinished. Where was the rest? Desperate and unwise, he had to know. No, he did not consider that there might be no more. No, he did not consider that even if Angela had never been lost, the album might still have been a fiction, that they might have quarreled, turned silent toward each other, divorced, that they might have faced the heart-ripping grief of a sick, suffering child. No. Shaken and intoxicated, the shoe man did not see the unfinished album as a hoax. He felt cheated of the pictures that should have filled the empty pages. He knew what they were. Happy birthdays, barefoot days at the beach, graduation with honors, a twenty-fifth wedding anniversary party, his daughter's white wedding and his grandchildren. So, where were they and where was Angela and where was all the time he'd lost?

Buddy knew. The shoe man was sure of it. His gifted

fingers, his once obedient friends, failed him as he dislodged
Buddy's business card from its clip. They fumbled like five
clumsy sausages with no bone, no muscle, no connection to
his brain. The card fluttered to the floor, turning itself over
and over again as it drifted downward, flying away from him
as he grabbed after it. He stomped it with his shoe. Kneeling, he triumphantly scraped the card off the linoleum with
a black fingernail. Shoving the maroon album under his
shirt, where it would be safe as long as he was safe, he forced
himself to lock the shop door and check it before he scuttled
to the corner telephone booth to demand his rights.

"Hello, Jack," Buddy answered. He knew who it was.
Who else would it be? "Are we ready to talk about a little
swap?" Buddy was ready. He had what he needed.

"I'm going to report you," the shoe man shouted.

"Report me for what?"

"For kidnapping."

"Kidnapping?" Buddy laughed. "I wasn't even born
when your Angela walked out on you."

The shoe man nearly threw down the album in rage. Who
was this devil? What did he want? "You son of a . . ."

"For all you know I could be your son."

"I didn't have a son."

"That's right. I gave you a daughter."

"I'll report you for harassment."

"Why don't you ask her?"

The shoe man swiveled toward the sidewalk. This was the sidewalk he knew on the Flatbush he'd always worked on. He could see the clock tower. It was eight fifty-three at night. His heart was still beating. He could hear it in his throat.

"My angels first," Buddy continued calmly, almost kindly. "Angela for the angels. Fair enough."

"Go to hell." The shoe man's curse was drowned out by a silent undercurrent of yearning. Jack heard the quaver in his voice betray forty years of wanting, and wanting to know, and he was shocked by it. He wasn't even safe from himself.

Buddy heard his will buckle. "I got a better idea," he replied.

That night, the shoe man missed visiting hours at the Harbinger Clinic.

When the shoe man telephoned Lucille to say he wasn't coming, his voice sounded unfamiliar. "I was worried to death," she said. Careless words.

"Lucille, would you . . ." The shoe man didn't know how to ask his next question. "I, uh . . ."

"What? Anything. What?"

"Uh, would you mind if I, uh, borrowed tomorrow's roses? It's not important."

In her happiness, Lucille forgot her pain and sat straight up in bed. "Oh that Buddy . . . I wanted to . . . He didn't

even . . . Well, I guess he was so . . . The main thing is
. . . Yes! Take all my roses. Oh, Jack, I can't believe it."

"Neither can I," said Jack. "But I do."

"What about . . ."

"The angels?"

"He can forget about the angels. It was *my* money."

"Your money?"

"Shit. I wasn't going to say. It doesn't matter. The main
thing is . . ."

"What money?"

"For the detective."

Lucille, his angel, had tried to spare him Buddy's price.
"Oh, Lucille." He couldn't tell her. What were the angels,
the shoe man thought, if he had his Angela and he had
sweet, foolish Lucille. What were the angels except his life's
work? "Lucille, Lucille, Lucille."

"I'm just so happy. Everything's so perfect."

"Yeah," said Jack. And then he wept and heaved in the
darkness where no one could see him. Avoiding shadows and
doorways, he scurried along the curb from streetlight to
streetlight, carefully scanning the sidewalks and passing cars
for anyone who might stop him and steal the album, stop
him and shoot him, stop him and demand his money, demand his money and, upon finding his wallet thin, shoot him
dead. He wouldn't resist. He wouldn't fight. In terror, he

would yield to fate. What else could he do? And if a jeep should jump the curb, what else?

But no one leapt at him and no one ran him over and though he spent a haunted night in the company of his angels and his past, he wasn't grateful to see the dawn.

As the shoe man showered, he thought not of Angela or Lucille but of Leopoldine and her money coat. Miracles happened. Why not? But he hadn't seen Leopoldine since that day. After miracles happened, what happened next? Would he take Angela in his arms and kiss her? Would she weep as he had done the night before? Would she tell him what happened the day she disappeared down the steps in her ankle-high boots and where she'd been ever since and why she hadn't come home to his arms and how she'd been faithful to him as he'd been faithful to her for forty years of enduring love?

And what would he say to her? How would he begin? With I missed you? With I love you? With why? With how?

He put on a yellowing, laundered shirt, his wedding shirt, and the tie Lucille had given him. He combed his hair with a watered comb, and last, he shaved. Holding his breath, he scraped the lime-scented Gillette from his face as if, if only he wielded his razor just right, all the age and sorrow would wash down the drain with the stubble-peppered foam. Why not?

He wasn't altogether sure he wanted this reunion. What

would it mean, after forty years, to see her again? What was next? What did it matter? He tried to touch his cheek as Angela might do, to rehearse her tender recognition, but it was his fingers doing the touching and his cheek doing the feeling. If he wanted to know her hand on his face again before he died, he had to see her, and if he saw his own dear Angela, held her hand against his face, felt the texture of her hair, what would anything else matter ever again?

ANGELA

fter the shoe man was gone, there were those who chose to disbelieve even what was thought to be known of his life. Had there ever been an Angela? Was she his Beatrice and not his wife? Was she ever more than a vision? Who knew? It didn't make sense. There were records, yes, but where were the facts? the proof? they would ask. Well, where?

Where? The shoe man didn't know. It was hard to believe with the stakes what they were, he agreed to a blindfold. But he did. Why? Because either he wore a blindfold or Buddy didn't take him to see Angela. Simple.

As the shoe man rode for hours in the back seat of what smelled like a new car, listening to Buddy sing along to synthesized rock on the radio, the dark enclosure of his eyes was actually pleasant. It closed out distraction. The soft flannel safely closed him in with his thoughts. He was no longer able to contemplate the reunion. It was too close. When he tried to force himself to picture it, his imagination rebelled, filling his shut eyelids with bursts of light and, to his surprise, the finished image of his Lucille angel. Her wooden flesh held light like a pearl in the sunshine. Her breasts were full but not heavy, rosy at the tips. Her waist slid into her hips and her rounded stomach swelled at the front. It was a womanly belly, a belly with an unborn baby inside, a secret baby, a gift. He would carve the baby from ebony and hide it there. He would fit the wood with an invisible seam. No one, certainly not Buddy, would ever know he had implanted a growing child. And below the angel's belly he would carve a triangular garden where her full thighs met. He would carve it with his narrowest dia-mond-tipped blade under a magnifying glass and fill it with bees and hummingbirds and miniature roses in all phases of bloom. He saw how it would trail enticingly down her left leg and how he would paint the faintest white Cupids in the clouds of her dimpled buttocks, so faint that they would not be seen in a casual glance, so subtle they would seem to be a thought that occurred to the one who saw them, they would sit outside of memory, barely there at all. He would stain her lips with purple kosher wine so that lips that were tempted to touch hers would taste a sweetness, and he would set diamonds at the center of fire opals for her eyes. And the wings . . .

The car came to a stop and Buddy untied the shoe man's blindfold. When his eyes adjusted, he saw a McDonald's pavilion.

"I figured we'd stop for lunch," said Buddy as he released the blindfold and helped Jack out of the car. It was a silver-grey Honda. The license plate was from New Mexico, but Buddy led him away before he could memorize the numbers.

Golden Arches. Red trim. A U-shaped parking lot. A horrifying clown presiding over a jungle gym. Screaming children. What was here to tell him where they were? Buddy had warned him not to ask. They were somewhere he didn't know. The waitress had a slightly southern accent. But did that mean she was from the South or they were in the South? Who knew?

After they finished their Big Macs and fries, Buddy led the shoe man to the car and tied his eyes. Jack sipped a large, sweet Coca-Cola through a straw and tried to bring his vision of the finished angel back before his eyes. She would not come again, but he had seen enough to rejoice at the beauty of his vision even if he never had the chance to carve it into reality. He closed his eyes and rested. The blindfold pressed against his eyelids. He knew he was on his way to Angela. Until the car stopped a second time Jack was content.

When Buddy next removed the shoe man's blindfold, they were parked at the curb in a suburban housing development that rolled up and over modest hills and dribbled off into orchards. From what Jack could tell, the houses had not been newly planted over an old farm; they had been there for a while. Juniper hedges stood under the paned windows of all the houses he could see. They were cut square or round, but they all grazed the white trim and they were all thick grey-green and mature. There were oak trees nearly as tall as the tree in Mrs. Rice's garden in the middle of some lawns and younger maples marking almost every driveway. All the lawns were cut short, and as it was a weekday, early afternoon, the loudest sound Jack heard was the hurried scratch of squirrels scrambling after each other across a rooftop. "Nice. You could have a nice life here. Very nice. She's here, right?" Maybe she was a tired housekeeper for a prosperous family and went home to a shack. He could have provided, provided nicely. Every penny he'd spent on his angels, he would have spent on her. She would have had a real gold watch, a ruby ring, free time. It wasn't too late. "She lives here, right?"

"Exacto."

"How can she afford a place like this?" Had she married another man? Learned shorthand and become a career girl?

"We're going to drive by first, so as not to alarm her," said Buddy.

"She's not expecting me?"

"Best that way."

If she didn't know he was coming, then she would never know if he backed out now, gave up and went back to Brooklyn, back to life as he'd known it, almost as he'd known it. Maybe he'd come close enough. Maybe it was enough to know she lived a nice life, he hoped it was a nice life, here in a nice place in a nice house and no more. But if he stopped here, if he stopped and went home and left her to this niceness undisturbed and undisturbing, say he persuaded Buddy to tell him where they were, say he learned the name she went by, say he got hold of a new phone book once a year and checked it just to reassure himself she was still there, say one year he opened the book and her name had vanished from the alphabetized list, what then?

"Excited?" said Buddy, patting the seat beside him. "Come up front so you can see."

The shoe man pulled two tired-looking roses from the bouquet of twenty-four and unwrapped the wet paper towel that covered the thorny stems. He arranged the flowers, resting the buds in a spray at the bend of his elbow. He slid gently across the front seat and whispered, "I'm ready."

Buddy pulled a scrap of paper from his shirt pocket and consulted it, then he started the motor. The shoe man clutched the roses. He did not feel the thorns dig into his fingers. He was not aware of the blood. Buddy drove slowly along the serpentine road, twice turning the car round at cul-de-sacs. The shoe man was too nervous to count the rights and lefts. At Orchard Road, Buddy said, "Ah. Good," and began scrutinizing the uniform black mailboxes that lined the street. "Yes!" he hissed at number 26. "Here we are."

The shoe man stared at 26 Orchard Road and what he saw was a house almost exactly like the houses on either side of it. He was able to squeeze three words between his lips. "Where is she?"

Buddy started the car and drove on. When he turned off Orchard on to Apple Tree Lane, he said, "According to my information, she'll pull in in about five, ten minutes. We'll park across the street. Anyone asks, we're from the gas company, right?"

"Okay," said the shoe man. He looked down at his hands and felt the pain. Blood had dripped on his clean shirt and trousers. What would Angela think? "Oh my God," said the shoe man. "I don't know . . . Maybe we should . . ."

Buddy handed him a paper tissue. "It's you she'll be looking at, not a couple little spots. You hand her the roses when you come to the door. You go slow. When I tell you. Not before. We don't want anyone having a heart attack. You say, shall we say, something simple. Hello. Hello, Angela. Something like that. And the rest will be, shall we say, history."

"You think?" It occurred to the shoe man that the most important person in his life was Buddy Lomax, himself, at least for the next three hundred seconds. Maybe he'd been too hard on Buddy.

"Sure." Buddy smiled and patted his shoulder.

The shoe man reached into his trouser pocket and removed his wallet. There were three photographs encased in plastic, one of Lucille before she'd done her nose and two of his beloved Angela. One then. Red lips, sea storm eyes, and freckles. One now. Different. Older. Pale blonde. Tan and slender. Buddy had given him these pictures. Buddy had given him a past. Maybe Buddy wasn't so bad.

She drove a bright red Toyota past the maple and parked outside the garage. He saw her scotch-blonde hair. The shoe man lurched forward. Buddy thrust an arm across his chest. "Wait."

She let herself out the driver's side. She wore red nail polish. A gold ring. Was it the ring he had given her on their wedding day? She was wearing a golf visor and a red pleated skirt. A golf skirt, not the right color but in all other ways the same as the skirt in the picture. Blonde hair cut short. Her legs were tanned, exactly. Time had been kind to her. No varicose veins. She wore gleaming red kid flats, high-grade leather, leather soles. The right shoes for a shoe man's wife. She opened the back door and bent over the seat. Her hair swung over her face before he could see it. He held his breath. Her face, that would be the test. But did he need a test? No. He needed Angela. Angela. His angel. His lost life, his love.

She emerged hugging two brown grocery bags to her bosom. Oh, how he remembered being where those bags were. She wore sunglasses, black, round, stylish Jackie O sunglasses that shaded her eyes and the bridge of her nose. Her cheeks. Where were Angela's cheeks? These were the cheeks of a dead woman. He damned himself. How could he think it? They were white, purple and blue where they had once been a brown-speckled pink. The only pink he saw spread across her face in irregular blotches. Even from across the street he could see it wasn't influenza or fatigue that made her pale, it was scarring. Buddy read his mind. "I didn't want to tell you. Skin cancer."

"My poor, poor Angela," the shoe man intoned, wishing he could have been there, holding her hand in the hospital, assuring her he would always be there, aching because he had done none of these things, hating himself for unknowing neglect. He should never have slowed, no, stopped, his active search. He should have devoted his life, given up his shop. What were shoes? What was his business, his craft, his art? Who needed angels? Angela had suffered and he had failed to comfort her.

Before Buddy could restrain him, he jumped out of the car. Angela yelped and the groceries scattered. "No! No!"

said the shoe man, proffering his roses with one hand as he scrambled to gather Clorox, toilet paper, and oat bran with the other. There was something in his voice that told her there was no reason for fear.

"Why . . ." She hesitated. He looked into her deeply marred face, seeing his nineteen-year-old bride. The adoration that showed made her look away shyly. She had once been a beauty. "Why, roses." She knew what she was now. "Thank you."

The shoe man chased across her lawn to recover a cantaloupe. He returned, panting and eager, placing the fruit in her grocery bag with a sigh. "Thank you," she said again.

"You're very welcome," he answered. He stared at his empty hand, searching for words in the blackened lines of his palm. Finding nothing there, he dared look once again at her face. Was it tenderness he saw there? Recognition? Curiosity? Pity? "I wonder . . . Uh. The roses are for you."

She tilted her head so far to the side that her ear nearly touched her shoulder, studying Jack's face in much the same careful way Angie the parrot would do. "Thank you."

"From me." He reached toward her arm but drew back before he touched her. "Angela . . ."

Her lips tightened and an array of wrinkles formed a hard star around her mouth. "I'm afraid," she said. Was it sorrow in her voice? Anger? "I don't think you have . . ." She held out the roses to Jack. He shoved his hands in his pockets.

"Angela!" Jack insisted. "It's Jack. Me. Your Jack. Please remember. Oh, please." Poor Angela. Her confusion told him all. She must have been hit on the head or fallen. A shock. Forgetfulness. That had to be why she'd never returned. That had to be why. He would help her. He would bring it back. All the love. "Darling, poor darling. 1951. The red-topped table. Slippery devil. My shop. The park. Flat-bush. Remember the bar on Flatbush and Vanderpole. It's gone, now. But I still have the bed. And it still squeaks. I mean, not that I . . . Angela. Remember how we . . ."

"I'm sorry." She shook her head slowly from side to side. She tried to hand the roses back to Jack. "These aren't for me. I wish they were." He shoved his hands deep into his pockets. "I'm really sorry."

"No!" Jack tore the glasses from her face. Those eyes. They were her eyes. He was sure they were her eyes. "An-gela! Know me. Please. Look in my face. It's still me. I'm just old. I'm an old man. Oh, Angela. My whole life . . ."

"Look." Angela turned to Buddy for the first time. "Tell your friend to settle down," she growled, "or I'll call the police."

"Jack, take it easy," Buddy said halfheartedly.

Jack wept. He shook. His head flew back and he whirled on the lawn, his arms flailing until he fell, gasping, onto the green, scratching his face on the juniper.

The woman's eyes reddened. Tears magnified her scars as

they skated down the wrinkle grooves to the corners of her mouth. She touched her tongue to the salt. "I'm so sorry. Please." She pulled a carton of juice from her grocery bag and opened it. Kneeling beside the fallen man, she put the paper spout to his lips and he drank desperately, his hand gripping hers.

She did not pry his hand away, but she refused to meet his thirsty gaze. "Maybe you should get your friend to a doctor," she said to Buddy. "He's not well."

The shoe man dared not cease his drinking, afraid it would end the encounter, afraid he'd bungle, afraid, more afraid than he'd been since she was lost to him the first time.

"Me and my late husband, Will, we been here since our last boy was in college," she said, leaning close to his ear. "I don't know you, Jack."

The shoe man did not believe her words and he did not understand why she would lie. How could he prove she was who he knew her to be and not who she said she was?

If she was his Angela and she knew him and she lied, if she didn't want him, what was the point in proving anything?

If she was his Angela and had no memory of him, she also had no memory of his love.

And if she wasn't . . . No. He could not bring himself to think it.

The shoe man moaned like a lion shot in the flank, destined to bleed to death slowly, without hope of rescue.

e will return to the shoe man's devasta-
tion, but first, let's take a look at Lucille. Her
healing proceeded nicely, and once the bandages were off
and a hairstylist was smuggled into her room, it didn't take
long for the word to leak out. It took even less time for the
press to take the word and alter it into a sensation. You may
recall hearing something about the reporter who was arrested climbing the clinic walls. Yes, he was arrested, but no
one pressed charges.

He got photos, photos so good his colleagues cried
fake.

And he got the story he wanted, not that he actually had
to climb walls to do it.

THE TRUTH CAN BE TOLD. Marilyn Monroe's death was a HOAX. Secret sources admitted Miss Monroe was ALIVE and there was PROOF at the famed Harbinger Clinic, where she was installed for a minor facelift. The death of JFK had been STAGED so that the LOVERS could live in GLORIOUS SIN in an unnamed tropical island LOVE NEST.

And so on.

Lucille could not have been more delighted, unless. Unless she had heard from the shoe man. It wasn't fair for him to run off with Angela without so much as a fare-thee-well. It just wasn't right. And though Buddy tried to comfort her, her moment of greatness, her magnificent triumph, was tainted.

Where was Jack? Buddy urged her to try and understand. He talked about the way a man could be carried away, but if Jack had been carried away, why hadn't he dropped a quarter to call and share his happiness? It just wasn't right. He wasn't the type to abandon her one two three. She needed him now, now more than before.

Where was he?

Buddy and Marilyn checked into the Plaza's honeymoon suite. Not the one that you would check into if you spent your wedding night at the Plaza, the one the Duchess of York would get without having to ask. And when Tony Curtis, who happened to be in New York for an opening, passed through the lobby, stopped, gasped, bowed low at the waist, kissed Lucille's hand and backed through the revolving doors, shaking his head, pulling his ear, speechless, the management took note.

What the management didn't know was that as soon as Curtis had backed down the carpeted stairs, Lucille bent toward Buddy and whispered, "Who's that old man?"

Oh well.

The management, of course, had heard of the Marilyn imitator, had laughed amongst themselves when she reserved a room in that implausible Marilyn voice, but if Tony Curtis bowed . . .

All the extras an ordinary citizen would scrimp to pay for, all the extras Lucille had desired without quite knowing what they were, came to their door free, compliments of the management. Champagne. Oysters. Steak au poivre. It turned out she didn't like bubbles at the back of her throat, oysters felt like rubber in her mouth and the crunchy pepper stuck between her teeth. Even these disappointments could not dim her pleasure. If she didn't like what she was served, she could have something else. And she did. Chocolate mousse tasted like divine revelation. She licked the crystal goblet clean and ordered another. Marilyn Monroe was not some skinny stick model. She was a woman with womanly flesh.

Lucille was a woman with womanly flesh. She was Marilyn Monroe. She felt Marilyn or what she thought Marilyn would feel. When the door buzzer called her into the hall, she found roses and roses and roses and roses, four dozen roses at very least, spread at her feet and covered with a white card. *Undying love,* it said. She wondered whether her mystery fan knew everywhere she went, every time she sat with a magazine on a toilet seat, every time she cleaned the dirt from under her nails. And she understood why Marilyn disguised herself. Lucille lowered the puffy silk shade on the bathroom window before she undressed and ran a bath.

English stephanotis oil sat in a blue vial on the edge of the bath, next to the little French soap and the little natural loofah and the little French shampoo. She poured the oil in the water. It made her dizzily drunk on scent and it didn't bubble. "How classy can you get?" she murmured to herself. "I could get used to this," she called to Buddy.

"You will." He was waiting for her on the queen-size bed in a paisley satin dressing gown.

Lucille intended to make him wait.

Way back, back before Lucille Bixby had decided she was going to be famous, she'd known herself as a prison from which she longed to escape. And now, it seemed, she was free.

Lucille Bixby had needed Buddy Lomax.

Marilyn watched the oil rainbows swirl around her ribcage. Her sides were still swollen and yellow from bruising, but if she took enough Tylenol 3, they hardly hurt. And Buddy promised he would get her morphine, which, she had learned to her joy, detached her from pain entirely.

She sang, " 'Buffalo gals, won't you come out tonight? Come out tonight? Come out tonight? Buffalo gals, won't you come out tonight and dance by the light of the moon?' " And then she sang it all over again. She didn't care if Buddy grew impatient. It was and always had been Marilyn Monroe's right and privilege to expect a man to wait, to expect him to want her utterly whenever she appeared. And Buddy Lomax had waited for Marilyn Monroe all his life. She could be sure of his love. *He* needed *her*, now. Or so she thought.

Lucille patted the heavy white terry over her breasts. She felt her fingers and she felt the terry on her fingers, but her breasts felt nothing. They were still numb. She dabbed at her waist. The staples were out but the scar still felt knotty and raw. Lucille poured herself a glass of French water and swallowed an extra pill. She knew what was next. She didn't want any postsurgical twinges to come in the way of her long-awaited ecstasy. Lucille applied her Marilyn makeup and dabbed her beautiful numb bosom with Chanel No. 5. She tied her robe loosely and *emerged*.

If only Buddy's excitement hadn't expressed itself in an overeager spurt the instant he beheld the droplets of water that gathered over the naked oil-polished body of Miss Marilyn Monroe.

If only Lucille weren't numb in most of the places she wasn't sore.

If only Buddy hadn't been desperate to regain an erection and penetrate Miss Marilyn Monroe, perhaps he might have managed to remain where he wanted to be without withering.

If only Lucille hadn't grown so unused to unhampered sexual gratification that she'd lost the knack of yielding to her senses.

If only Buddy hadn't called her frigid, just like Marilyn.

If only Lucille hadn't pointedly thanked him for her stifled and aching condition, popped out her contact lenses, and gone to sleep thinking of Jack, yearning for Jack, praying for Jack.

If only she had cracked her eyes and seen Buddy's sleep-walking silhouette approaching the open window that overlooked an empty Fifth Avenue. If only. If only she had pushed him out.

If only Buddy hadn't awakened early, erect and savage.

If only Lucille had had time to put her contact lenses in before Buddy had her and had her and had her and then scrutinized what he had had, for Marilyn was a what and not a who to him.

If only Lucille hadn't understood by the look on his face that what it meant to be Marilyn was what it meant to feel the tip of a knife on your chest above your beating heart: vulnerable, incurably alone.

If only, in his damp postcoital repose, Buddy hadn't searched to discover the one thing that wasn't quite perfection.

If only he hadn't seen Lucille's white plastic contact lens case on the night table, kissed her ear and then whispered,

"Your eyes still aren't her eyes, my love, but I have a friend . . ."

If only Lucille had been born what she had wanted to become, another person entirely.

Ah, if only.

ucille slipped through the Plaza lobby wearing no makeup. She hunched over the pay phone receiver as she dialed the shoe man's telephone number one more time. The phone rang and rang, as it had done every time she'd tried to contact him, but this time, after the sixth ring, someone picked up. Picked up and put the phone down again without speaking. Lucille knew it was Jack. It had to be Jack. Without a word to Buddy, she wrapped her hair in a kerchief, disguised her eyes behind black glasses and ran the half block to the subway station. In the train, she could relax. How far she'd come from the days when sitting amongst so many black faces made her tremble and await the worst. She didn't notice them now. And they paid no attention to her.

Lucille ran up the cement subway steps toward Reliable Repair. The metal gate was up. Lucille stumbled and grabbed the rail. "Jack!" she called, though she couldn't see him through the dusty window. "Jack!" Shoes were scattered on the bench. Dead Angie the parrot eyeballed the sidewalk. The *Post* was folded on a shoeshine chair. Lucille tried the door. It was locked. She jiggled the handle and tapped the glass. "Jack!" she shouted, then she saw his mail piled in a heap on the floor below the slot and she knew he hadn't been to the shop since Angela. Could a woman do that to a man? A wife? Would he leave his shop unprotected for days just to be with her? *That* was love. Pretty stupid, she thought as she yanked the protective gate across the face of Reliable Repair, pretty crazy. But that was love, she said to herself, true love.

Lucille removed her kerchief and glasses before she entered Gloria's Pizzeria. She wanted them to know her face but she forgot that her face had been so altered that her face wasn't her face anymore. "I'd like a slice and have you seen Jack around?" she blurted.

"One sly." One of the Albanians opened the oven and slid a cold slice toward the back. His fellow employees, his countrymen, argued in Albanian, but Lucille knew what they were saying. "Marileen Munvroe."

"Have. You. Seen. Jack? The. Shoe. Man. Reliable. Repair. How. Long. Gone? Where. Is. Jack?" she asked, patiently saying each word and letting it stand before saying the next.

The Albanians continued to babble. If they understood what she was saying, they didn't think it important to answer.

"Jack! Jack!" she yelled.

Gloria tumbled out of the kitchen a mess. Vic stood beside her, his shirt half buttoned. "What the hell's goin' on?"

"Have you seen the shoe man?"

Gloria pushed her hair away from her face and twisted it up as she stared at Lucille. "Anyone ever tell you you could be Marilyn Monroe's twin sister?"

"I need to find him."

"Aren't you his little friend?"

"I thought maybe you might . . ."

"Well, he doesn't check in with me since you came along, sugar plum." Gloria licked her lips and leaned against Vic's chest.

Lucille left without her slice, cursing herself and her hollow head. Why had she bothered with Gloria when all she had to do was march down Parker, let herself in and see for herself?

She'd give him an earful, she would. I've been upside down with worry. How could you? And then she remembered Angela. I've heard so much about you. But what if they were in bed? Did people that old do those things? Not more than once. They'd had plenty of time. And anyways . . . She hesitated at the front door. It wasn't Angela she was afraid of. It was something she couldn't name. Something about the way he'd left the shop. Maybe he was dead. Maybe he'd died in passion. Maybe they both had. Or maybe it was worse. What was worse?

She saw the dead and dying roses piled on Jack's doormat. Why hadn't the landlady cleared them off? Why hadn't Jack? She pushed them away and tried to look under the crack beneath the door. The hallway was black. She heard no sound at first. Listening past the apparent stillness, she found another sound, a rhythmic ticky scratching, barely audible. She knew what it was. Metal on wood. She'd heard the sound nights when she lay in bed. It was the shoe man. He was working. If he was working, he was alive, but where was Angela?

For some reason, she didn't know why, Lucille removed her shoes before she inserted her key in the lock.

WHAT LUCILLE
DIDN'T KNOW

Shoes on. Shoes off. It didn't make any difference. Though her key fit the lock, the door didn't open.

Lucille suspected something had gone wrong with the reunion. She didn't suspect anything vile. Just something sad, something that might have sent the shoe man on a bender. Men went on benders, didn't they, when love went cockeyed? She'd never known a man to actually do this, but that was what men did on television and she'd watched one hell of a lot of television at the Harbinger Clinic.

Lucille had no way of knowing what had happened that day. Because the shoe man couldn't bear to tell her, she didn't even know that Buddy had demanded the angels. And she certainly had no idea that during a long, silent ride back to Brooklyn in the company of Buddy Lomax, the shoe man had sworn he would never part with his angels alive. His angels were his life. His proof that he had lived. That there had been a life, without Angela, without a family, without birthdays and weddings and graduations and grandchildren, but a life, his own life.

Buddy didn't know that, either. He had loaded the lowing, semiconscious shoe man into the silver-grey Honda and driven for hours. When the shoe man stirred, Buddy said, "You okay?" and the shoe man didn't answer. Then he said, "Man, I'm really sorry. You really zeroed out on that one. I told you go slow, but who the hell knows? When it comes to people . . ." When the shoe man still didn't answer, he added, "Welp. That's life. But a deal's a deal." He might have guessed what the shoe man was thinking, but it made no difference to him. The magnificent jewel-eyed angels were his and he would have them. He would have them, and when the time came, he'd sign them. He could wait. And he would wait. When the time was right, the world would say his name in the same breath as Michelangelo's. The world would celebrate the angels as his and his acclaim would not be limited to the transformation of a mousy mortal into the radiant Miss Monroe. He would go down in history. He would be in the Metropolitan Museum. The Vatican. And every major magazine in the world. The shoe man was just a tool, a hand attached to a knife. The angels were his.

"Marilyn's out on Monday, so I'll bring a van round this weekend. You just have the stuff off the walls. I'll crate it up. Don't you worry. Loving hands the whole way, Jack. Couldn't have found a better home."

"Okay," he lied. Lying would give him time. And time he needed. Time he'd wasted. All his life? Had he wasted all his life waiting for Angela, for the moment past, for this unspeakable present?

No. Again, his angels strengthened him. They came to him, the seraphim, cherubim, the many-eyed chariots, dominions, virtues and powers, the principalities, angels and archangels.

Raphael took his arm when he was too weak to walk; Gabriel whispered in his ear. Secret words in an angel tongue. The shoe man panicked. What was Gabriel saying to him? What? And then, yes, he understood. With strength from the heavens, he walked to the corner bodega. From the gun running Yemenites he bought a *Post*, some M&M's, and, at Raphael's silent urging, he asked for a pistol. The Yemenite said, "No pistol here," but the shoe man knew better. Everyone did. He put fifty dollars on the counter and the Yemenite passed him the gun and its bullets and the M&M's in a brown bag. And then, Raphael led him to the Koreans. There, he bought cans of soup and cans of beans and cans of clams and cans of tuna and cans of juice and cans of corn and cans of pineapple and cans of peanuts and cans of coffee and carried the heavy packages home without feeling the weight.

Alone with his angels, alone forever with no intruders, no love, no loss, no agony, no one, he would have peace. Alone, he would finish his work, his last angel, and she would be queen and there would be no other. No Angela. No. There was no Angela. No Lucille. No. There was no Lucille. She was a dream. A headache. A fever. A curse. He pushed the dresser down the hall and against the locked door to his apartment. And then the angels blessed him with a thick, dreamless, sleep.

Lucille knew nothing of any of this. And Lucille did not know that while she was still confined, watching *Guiding Light* in a morphine haze, Buddy had arrived with a rented van and packing blankets, just as he promised. Lucille couldn't have known that when Buddy pounded the door, the shoe man fired two shots at it, and that, though the bullets were too soft to penetrate the fireproof metal, and though they did what they were intended to do and made Buddy Lomax go away, they had a dangerous and unintended effect.

Neither Lucille nor the shoe man knew that, inspired by the sound of gunshot, Buddy returned to his Hell.

But what Lucille did know was that when she turned the key, the door refused to open past three quarters of an inch. She put her eye to the opening and saw the dresser in the way. And then she saw Jack, unshaven and naked, panting as he slid his back along the wall toward the door with a pistol in his hand. "Jack, it's me," she said. She spoke in a soothing voice, drawing again on what television had taught her about what people did when guns were pointed at them. "It's okay. Lucille's home now. Everything's okay. Now, put it down. Lucille loves you. Now put down the gun."

Raphael told him to shoot but the shoe man knew that angels could err, err and fall. "I can't shoot," he answered. "That's Lucille."

"It's Lucille," Lucille said. "Lucille loves you."

"Lucille loves me." Jack loved Lucille. Raphael said shoot! You can't trust her. Look what she's done. "I don't trust you," said Jack.

"I'm sorry, Jack. I'm really sorry. Let me in. I'll make us some nice muffins. Some nice hot blueberry muffins."

Jack put the gun on top of the dresser and moved toward the door. "Where is he?"

"Who?"

"You know who."

"I'm all alone."

"I'll kill him."

"He's not here." Lucille slid her hand sideways through the crack in the door, hoping Jack would take it and feel her love and her warmth. Jack studied her fingers. They were the angel's fingers.

"You're my angel."

"Yes. I'm your angel. Let me in."

"But you're already here."

"Yes. I'm here. And I'll protect you."

Again Raphael told him to shoot, but he wasn't listening to Raphael now. "She said she didn't know me."

"No," Lucille answered. "Maybe she just . . ." Jack's body crumpled as if all the bone underneath had dissolved into his flesh. Hunched in a ball on the wooden floor, he titled his head back and howled a long, silent symphony of grief. Lucille wanted to run from the sight of his misery. So great and naked was his pain that she would have traded her life for an end to it. "Oh, Jack. I'm sorry. Oh, Jack. I'm so sorry. It's all my fault. I'm so sorry," she intoned. "Jack, I'm so sorry."

She didn't hear the police creep up beside her. She screamed when Officer Couch grabbed her shoulder and pulled her from the door. She screamed and kicked and cried. Couch held her arms behind her back. She thrashed from side to side, shouting, "Leave him alone! Leave him alone!" and he handed her to a young black cop with a shiny, expressionless face who carried her, sobbing, out of the building.

Lucille didn't see four cops heave the door open, smashing the shoe man's dresser against the wall. She didn't see the pistol fall from the dresser and spin across the floor or hear Officer Ullman bark, "Freeze!" to the petrified shoe man.

She didn't hear Ullman read Jack his rights or see the shoe man dirty himself on the floor from the fright. Lucille never witnessed the way a man he'd never seen dragged him into the shower and sprayed him down with icy water. Lucille wept in the back of the patrol car, not knowing that the pelting brought the shoe man back to himself, that he snatched a towel Lucille had bought on sale to match the bathroom tiles, that he covered his nakedness, aware of it for the first time since his angels had come to save him.

She didn't see Couch cuff the shoe man's hands behind his back and force his legs into his green chinos, catching his pubic hairs in the zipper as he yanked it up. She didn't hear the shoe man yelp.

And how could she have known that the angel Raphael said not to worry, that Gabriel told him he would not be alone, that no matter what happened next, the angels would protect him? And what would she have thought if she had known?

The shoe man smiled. If only Lucille had seen him smile, she might have had a glimpse into the secrets of surviving this life that those who suffer most know best.

If only.

Lucille phoned Buddy from the precinct. He wasn't at the Plaza. He wasn't home. She found him at The Agency and begged him for help.

If only she had known that it was he who had called the police to report a madman with a gun,

that it was he who had generated a grainy photo of Jack leaning out his back window with an AK-47 in his arms,

that it was a cinch to animate the image backward and forward so that it was no longer still, so that Jack opened the window, lifted the gun, leaned toward the oak tree in the mass murderer's yard and fired,

that he had clouded the image, and blued it true to night, and transferred it to poor-quality video so that it would look amateurish,

and that it was he who anonymously mailed the video cassette to the precinct, knowing it would cause the shoe man's arrest for the unsolved murder of his neighbor, Mr. Heinz,

everything might have been different.

But Lucille didn't know any of these things.

Buddy told Lucille to cooperate with the police and he would do whatever he could, which, as you will see, he did.

The video was damning but not definite. The images
were faint and dark. They would have to be bumped
up and studied. But the shoe man was in possession of an
unlicensed gun. Even though it was the wrong gun, possession was a crime and they booked him on it.

It was just in the course of searching the premises that
Kelley opened the back room door. No one had warned him.
Truth was, they'd been so busy subduing the startled shoe
man that they hadn't got past the bedroom. Kelley crossed
himself, averting his eyes in reverence and confusion. He
looked back over his shoulder, but decided not to call the
other officers quite yet. He wanted this vision to himself, so
his eyes could see all of it, all of the jewel-eyed angels in near

flight, their heads inclined to listen, their lips near a whisper. Maybe he would hear what it was they wanted to say. If this was heaven, he no longer feared death. What his late mother wouldn't have given to pray at the feet of these blessed angels, and here they were, here on Parker Street off Flatbush, sixteen blocks from his late mother's house, and here, in their midst, was the Virgin Mary herself. But no, he looked in her face and his eyes did not burn. This was no virgin. Voluptuous. Unchaste. He knew the face. A seductress. It was . . . It didn't come to him easily, in the company of the glittering heavenly host. It was . . . He'd been in the precinct too long to linger in awe. There was no heaven on earth. It was some kind of Marilyn Monroe. Monroe, only holy, an angel of sex, who pulled him toward her like a magnet. He touched the wood tenderly. Captain Kelley felt his body stir. "Hail Mary, Mother of God," he began. He touched the angel again. He touched her burgundy lips. They were cool and velvety and suddenly Kelley feared again, feared for his soul and his sanity. "In here!" he shouted gruffly.

Ullman arrived first. "Pretty incredible, huh?"

"You've seen this?"

Ullman didn't answer.

"He goddamn warehouses a fortune in fuckin' holy art and you don't fuckin' report it. Book him."

And so the shoe man was also booked for the theft of the

angels. Kelley didn't know whose angels they were and Kelley didn't know when or where they had been stolen. As Kelly saw it, that was a technicality. It was plain to him that the shoe man's motive for the murder of Heinz was discovery. Heinz must have had the dope on him. Heinz must have known about the angels. Maybe he wanted money. Who knew?

The shoe man took Gabriel's advice and said nothing. He did not ask for a lawyer. When the court assigned him one, he did not speak to him. If he had anything to say, he said it to the angels in his head. He could trust them.

Lucille, however, had already spoken once too often. Ullman recalled his first visit to the shoe man. Lucille swore she had been at home with the shoe man at the time of the shooting. Now she said that on that night three black children had trampled her on the sidewalk as they ran from who knew what. "Why couldn't it be them?" she argued.

Couch reamed the inside of his ear with a pencil eraser. The girl looked different than before. Different in a big way. She looked like Marilyn Monroe. Exactly. What the hell did a blonde like her want with a crazy old man? "Did you see their faces, honey?"

"It was dark."

"It was dark. Right. And they were young, male and black. Good. Good. There's a lead for you. Ever seen a polar bear in a snowstorm? We have a problem here, honey, because if you were with the suspect all night and you were being mowed down by three kids with no faces, then either you got special magical powers or you're lying, right, honey?"

"Can I see him please?"

"Not tonight," said Ullman. "And maybe not tomorrow. Did anyone ever tell you you look just like Marilyn Monroe?"

"You really think?" Lucille opened her lips so the cop could see the tip of her tongue. "Maybe I can just say a little hello?" She ran her hands along the curve of her new breasts. "Just for a little minute?" She crossed her legs so her skirt would sneak up her thigh. "Pretty please?"

It had to be sex. "Why?"

"I told you. He's my very good friend."

Ullman was in hot with Kelley. He didn't need any more trouble. "Well, your very good friend is going to have to sleep all alone tonight and I'm happily married, so why don't you run along home?"

Where was home?

Lucille returned to the Plaza Hotel, locked herself in her suite and ordered a beer and a turkey club. She took three Tylenol 3s, which, she observed, made Tylenol 9 but which did nothing to remove the pain that had become her whole self. That's all I am, she thought. Marilyn Monpain. Everything I do turns out the opposite of what I meant and that's cause I'm stupid stupid stupid stupid stupid and now Jack's in jail. Poor Jack. And it's all my fault. All my fault cause I'm stupidupidupid stupoopoopid. I want to die, but I'm too chicken. If I died I'd be famous. Just like Marilyn Monroe. Only I'd be dead and I wouldn't know about it, and fuck everybody. My luck, I'd probably go to hell. Fault ault malt fault faultie faultie bo baultie, banana fanna fo faultie . . . Lucille turned on the television. She didn't want to go to sleep. Her thoughts were awful, but if the right show came on she could stop them. Her dreams. She was sick of dreams. She wanted to be safe. She cocooned herself in a pink wool blanket, rocking back and forth, staring hopefully at the flickering screen.

She was happy to see Buddy. Buddy held her. Buddy rocked her. Buddy said everything was going to be okay. Buddy had a surprise for her. A big surprise.

"A job?"

"A big job. But that's not it . . ."

"My eyes?"

"Yes, but that's not it either . . ."

Buddy had morphine. And that made her happy. There was no more pain until she saw the 11 P.M. news. Then even morphine couldn't help.

The simple hope of cracking a minor murder case in a city that swallows murders like multiple vitamins isn't news, if by news you mean what headlines with what pictures at six and eleven. We could ask why one man's murder is minor and another's major, but that isn't the point.

The point is, without the angels and the news, the Angel Carver might have spent the rest of his life sleeping on a concrete bed in a maximum-security prison.

Art historians from Bavaria, Avignon and Rome were flying to New York to identify the angels, which, it was assumed, were a secret hoard stolen from an aristocrat's chapel, a convent, a villa, a château or a schloss, during the

Second World War. Which chapel, convent, villa, château or schloss, no one knew, but Interpol was on the case. Who the master sculptor was and the era in which he worked was under debate. The wood, the jewels, the paint, would have to be analyzed. It was too soon for an answer, and the Renaissance expert at Sotheby's had refused early comment. When pressed by the television reporter, Officer Ullman confessed he'd always been suspicious, but then he didn't know art, he just knew what he liked, until Captain Kelley came along. Couch offered his cult theory and added a spy ring. "But I'll leave it to the experts," he said.

Stolen. How else to explain a room filled with angels, any one of which would have been a lesser artist's masterpiece?

But, you ask, couldn't they see it was the shoe man's workroom? What about the tools? What about them? The shoe man may have been possessed by his angels, but he was not untidy. When he finished his final angel, he scrubbed them and dried them in his oven, where they remained. Unfortunately, the angel room was pristine when Captain Kelley entered it.

On the screen, Lucille saw herself, herself as a radiant angel, with her eyes aglitter. What color were they? The image left the screen, replaced by the murder video.

Lucille knew she wasn't hallucinating by the horror on Buddy's face.

He had miscalculated. He had underestimated.

When the shoe man became dangerously uncooperative, Buddy Lomax developed his own safety plan and prepared a forged and back-dated bill of sale for his angels, assuming he could quietly claim them and hold them in obscurity for a few years, until the shoe man died or succumbed to his delusions, until there was no one who would or could contest his authorship. Now what? Art historians from Bavaria, Avignon and Rome. Now what? He should have expected they'd leak the video. Now what?

Lucille rolled her head weakly from side to side like a punctured wind sock. "Poor Jack. Poor, poor Jack."

"What about me?"

"Poor you." Lucille didn't understand. If poor Buddy, then poor everybody. Buddy had Marilyn Monroe and that was what he wanted, wasn't it? "Why poor you?"

"Shit, Marilyn. This is a fucking disaster," said Buddy.

"More tomorrow," promised the reporter.

"Poor poor poor Jack." Wanting nothing more than to shut her up, Buddy poured his creation, his drug-woozy Marilyn, a lemon vodka from the bar on which the TV rested. "Buddy sweetie, pretty please give Marilyn the telephone. She wants to call the news and tell them the truth. Gimme the phone, sweetie. Get me the operator. Call me the news, Buddy. Call me everybody. I'll tell them the truth. I'm an eyewitness." Buddy ignored what she said and poured her a scotch. Lucille closed her fingers around the tumbler and fell asleep before her lips touched the rim of the glass. Buddy watched the scotch dribble out of the tumbler, soaking the pillowcase on which she lay her head. He undressed and, aroused by her total helplessness, he took her, panting and thrusting, thrusting and heaving, heaving and sweating until he had emptied himself and he was limp with satiation.

All the while, she slept like the dead. She slept like the dead but she didn't die, and that was fine with Buddy.

For the time being.

MARILYN'S EYES

Buddy left the suite the next morning to buy a copy of the *Times*. He expected Lucille to sleep through the afternoon, but when he returned, she was gone.

Lucille had telephoned the reporter who printed the TRUTH about Marilyn Monroe with her pictures. She promised him a story so hot it would burn his fingers. He met her at Rumpelmayer's on Central Park South. They shared a sundae. He flirted with Marilyn. But when she told him what she knew of the shoe man and his angels, he said, "I'm sorry, honey. That's not a story. Unless . . . Did you have a love nest going? What about the JFK angle? Was he jealous?"

Lucille left him to pay the check.

She cried her way down Fifth Avenue without noticing the stir she caused. She didn't care about the poking and the pointing and the whispers. So what if they saw Marilyn Monroe? What good did that do her?

She had an idea. The statue. Anyone could see it was her. She ran to a telephone booth and called *Live at Five*. "That shoe man," she said. "The guy with the angels?"

"You have something?" said the intern.

"I can prove he carved those angels himself."

The intern handed the phone to the assignment editor. "Give me the number you're calling from."

"I'm calling from a phone booth, but you can reach me at the Plaza until tomorrow morning."

"What can you tell me?"

"One of the angels is me?"

"Which one?"

"The one . . ." Lucille didn't know how to put it. "The one that . . ." She plunged in. "The one that's Marilyn Monroe. It's me. I lived with him, see."

"You're Marilyn Monroe."

She paused. And hesitated. "My name is Lucille. Lucille Bixby. You can ask him. But now I'm Marilyn Monroe, well, I'm her except for my eyes, and I posed."

"You posed?"

"If you look at me you'll know."

"I see," said the assignment editor. "Well. Thank you for calling."

Lucille stared at the grey phone before laying it in its cradle. "Stupid jerk." She wondered how much it would hurt if she walked in front of a city bus. Then they'd pay attention. Then they'd realize. She didn't have the guts. She returned to the Plaza.

"Where the hell have you been, my little pussycat?" Buddy asked, almost singing the question. Her distress brought out the most stunning Marilyn flush, but she wasn't wearing her contacts. Those eyes.

"Trying to get someone to listen."

"And?" He kissed her eyes closed. Now, she was his girl. She whipped away, and there were those damned wrong eyes wide open. It grated. "You're not wearing your contacts."

"Screw my contacts."

"You're right. Poor child."

"No one the fuck believes me." Lucille punched a pink pillow that bore an impression of her head.

"Buddy has another present for his poor little itty bitty Marilyn." Buddy sat beside her on the bed and unclenched her fist. He pulled her forearm toward him, licking the white underside. He tested a vein with his forefinger, and Lucille obediently remade her fist. She needed a little taking away, a little heaven, a little death, a little morphine. "You just haven't found the right person to help you, little one," Buddy murmured as he gave her the shot, with a little extra. He had to stop her. Stop her, perfect her, make her wholly his, but not kill her. That wasn't necessary. Buddy had faith in history.

ucille didn't know where she was or how she'd got there, but her head felt like lead she knew she couldn't move and she felt a man's beefy breath steaming her cheek. She opened her mouth to speak, but she didn't hear her own voice. "Hold still, honeybunch," the voice with the breath said. "We're just about finito here."

Her eyes were open, but she couldn't see out of one and her other saw only close moving shadows. "My eyes!"

"We're doing your eyes, sweetheart. For a little pick-me-up." That was Buddy's voice. "And Marilyn, they put you over the top. You're not going to believe. Picture perfect. Awesome."

"Hold my hand." She stretched her fingers toward his

voice. "I'm scared," she said, and then she smiled. "Am I really perfect?"

"Totally." Buddy kissed her fingertips. "One hundred percent."

"One hundred and ten," said the beefy-breathed voice above her face. She'd never heard his voice before. She'd never hear it again. But there was something calming about it, and easy to trust. "Your eyes are as blue as blueberries at the rim and then, going in toward the pupil, I've got an autumn sky with a little chill in it," he said. He hadn't done eyes, but over the years he'd done every other part of the body. He was known for elaborate floral nipples and paisley penises. He'd even done dragon tongues for a few Japanese, without a single croaker. He was an artist. He was an expert. He saw no reason why eyes should be a problem, except for the probability of blindness. Blindness bothered him. His eyes meant more to him than his own untattooed penis. But his buddy Buddy said the blindness didn't matter, only perfection, and they weren't his eyes. He'd sterilized the needles with fire and hydrogen peroxide and boiled them twice. They were clean and sharp. They pierced the cornea easily. The iris received the color as well as could be hoped. There was no blue bleed into the whites. The tattoo artist had mixed the dye fresh himself, so he knew it was gentle and extremely pure. His hand was steady. "I'm going to finish up with some tiny flecks of silver. Just highlights, so you sparkle." He figured that a woman who was willing to chance the loss of her eyesight just to be the perfect physical duplicate of Marilyn Monroe deserved the best he could give her. It was a matter of respect.

He didn't have to do the best, but he did. He knew even his best was no guarantee. It never was. He always made his clients sign consent, even though tattooing was illegal. "It's a sue-crazy country," he'd tell them, "and God forbid . . ." But this girl, this goddess, seemed too far gone to care when she'd written MM, and Buddy said she had a little weakness for the fruit of the poppy. Oh well. Whatever happened, he couldn't be sued. And the price was right, with a little extra for his silence. He'd been on Forty-second Street for eighteen years. Eighteen years. Penises. Tongues. Nipples. Now eyes. He didn't know why people did what they did. They just did. Maybe in a few days she'd be able to look in the mirror and see how lovely she was. Maybe she'd have the luck. "Keep those baby blues out of the light for twenty-four hours at least. No peeking," he said as he taped sterile gauze over her stunning eyes. "God bless you, Marilyn. I always was a fan. Always loved you. And good luck."

Buddy slid her cat-eyed sunglasses over the bandages. Lucille clenched his arm for balance as he steered her through the door with his arm around her shoulder. They rode in a close elevator and crossed a lobby that led to the street. She inhaled the urine, gasoline, sweet hot cotton candy, popcorn, hot dogs and shish kebab, and swooned. "I can't see," she said. She felt sun on her face. "What time is it?" She swiveled her head from side to side as if somehow she could shake sight into her eyes. Buddy caught her chin and kissed her. Her lips were numb. "I don't feel anything."

"That's so it won't hurt," Buddy answered. "You're just dilated."

"What about Jack?"

"The best thing you can do is to settle into bed . . ."

"I don't want . . ."

"Doctor's orders. You heard. Anyways, the very best thing you can do for Jack, the only way you're going to help him, is not to go batshit. We'll settle you in at my place, where you can rest your eyes without any questions and you can tell me everything, every little detail. I'll write it down and we'll organize it up scientific so you can prove you know what you're talking about."

Lucille touched the adhesive tape that held the gauze to her temples. "I can prove about the angels 'cause I saw that with my own eyes, but the murder . . ."

"That could be rough, but one thing at a time," said Buddy as he helped her off the curb toward the growling grit-spitting street and into a taxi that smelled of fried chicken. There was so much to remember, Lucille forgot the present and its odors.

The dark shield of bandages, the stinging pain deep in her

head that was growing up and over the sweet, but diminishing, protection of morphine were less real to her than the night the shoe man gave up his bed to her, than the Chinese and the perked coffee and the muffins every morning. She was determined to remember every muffin she'd ever baked for him, every walk they'd taken together, everything he told her about his life, his wife and his angels, everything, so that she could tell Buddy. He could make them all listen to her. If they wouldn't listen to her, they'd listen to him. He had the knack. That was one of the things she sort of loved about Buddy Lomax, his knack.

LEOPOLDINE

eanwhile, there was Leopoldine. You remember Leopoldine? Mrs. Rice? The relatives? The pictures? The money-lined blonde mink coat?

Well, she went where the shoe man hoped she would go, to her home in the Islands. And where she lived, she was a wealthy, wealthy woman, whose money had a way of making money. She enjoyed her fortune and she enjoyed it without guilt because the money was a miracle, her miracle. Because miracles ought not go unappreciated, she became a religious woman and made sure the Lord knew she was grateful. She gave to the poor and she shared with her friends and she augmented the local minister's meager salary and she believed that there was justice in the world.

In order to keep believing in justice, Leopoldine did not own a television, nor did she read the newspapers. Thus it was practically another miracle that she heard about the fate of the shoe man who had been so very kind to her and oft missed dear, dear Mrs. Rice.

The Sunday after the shoe man's arrest, she arrived, as she always did, at the Church of the Heavenly Rest and seated herself in the second pew. It was Minister Debrill who chose the newly discovered Brooklyn angels for his sermon. "Holiness needs no adoring audience," he preached, "but can thrive in isolation, unseen and unapplauded. Nor does holiness yield to human weakness. No. Theft cannot taint the sacred beauty of the holy object stolen. And yet we must ask ourselves why a simple shoe repairman in the town of Brooklyn . . ." He had no idea of Brooklyn's size, having never been to America, himself. "We must ask ourselves what in his soul drove him not to prayer but to possession and thievery of these holiest and most divine of holy angels. To steal what has been consecrated unto God. Was it greed? Did he, do we all, yearn to clutch the idol to his bosom, forsaking the spirit? And what drove him to kill before the eyes of God in the sight of heavenly beauty come to earth? What? Day after day for nearly half a century, the murderous angel thief sat at the cobbler's bench, modestly repairing the shoes of those who were, perhaps, more prosperous than the proprietor of the simple shop he called Reliable Repair. Reliable.

And yet . . ." Minister Debrill nodded slowly in Leopoldine's direction. She often talked of Brooklyn and her friends there. There was nothing like Brooklyn anywhere but Brooklyn and as much as she loved the island of her birth, she yearned for a knish. "Yet, we must ask ourselves . . ." the minister continued, but Leopoldine's thoughts had left the sermon. She was listening to the Lord's message. And she knew it had come to her, directly to her, for no idle purpose. The Lord didn't waste his time.

It had to be her shoe man. And she knew in her soul, which was clean, that what the minister presented as fact was evil falsehood. There had to have been a terrible injustice done to her own friend of many years and kindnesses. Leopoldine was positive, she had no doubt, that he was neither a killer nor a thief, and that if holy angels were in his hands, the Lord himself had put them there. Minister Debrill didn't know the truth, and she burned to tell him so, but she forced herself to listen to his lies, praying he would speak the shoe man's name. Her prayer was granted. Leopoldine jumped up from the pew. "Praise the Lord!" she shouted.

She knew what she had to do. She took the blonde mink coat from its place in the closet, packed it and the sweaters she'd saved and boarded a plane for New York.

It will surprise you to know that twenty-four hours after Lucille's bandages were removed and Buddy beheld his Marilyn Monroe perfect in every respect, he married her.

Why? Why do you think? Don't mention love. Mention property and precaution. He was taking no chances.

When she was distressed that the world still showed itself to her only in shadows, Buddy comforted her with loving tenderness, promising her sight would return any day and almost meaning it. He combed her hair. He powdered her cheeks. With a gentle hand he smoothed her white eyeshadow over her lids and painted a perfect feather of black above her lashes. He dressed her and caressed her and brought her tea and morphine and listened to all she had to say about Jack. When he touched her, it was with a light hand, seeing to her pleasure before his own, her pleasure being his pleasure. He even drove her to the prison to visit the shoe man.

Why? By now you should know that Buddy always had his reasons.

Buddy drove Lucille to prison, and as she walked across the parking lot, all the prisoners blessed with a view called out to her from their cells offering to fuck her and suck her and so on. She gave the boys an easy breezy Marilyn wave and they doubled their offers and their volume.

The security guard who searched her purse for weapons personally escorted her and Buddy to the visitor's check-through point and stayed to watch her from behind as the check-through guard had her walk—if what she did with those legs and the friction between those thighs and those in and out up and down hips in that too tight skirt that held her edible bottom so, so close could be called walking—through the metal detector four times, each time ignoring the indication of metal in, not on, her person. Finally, he had to speak. "Did anybody ever tell you . . ."

Lucille turned her head toward the voice and tried to focus on the round shadow she took to be his face. "No, sweetie. You're the first." She giggled and offered him her wide red lips for a gander. "Any of the TV guys here, today, 'cause if there are, you tell them Marilyn wants to have a little press conference, won't you, handsome?"

"Sure," said the guard, but he assumed she was joking.

The angels told the shoe man not to leave his cell, but the guard, whose name was Willy, yanked him to his feet and pulled him down the corridor. "You're not going to want to miss this one, not where you're going," he said. "You get one of these, you go. You get one of these, you dream on it for the rest of your life. There are men who'd kill for . . ." Willy decided to shut up. The shoe man didn't cause trouble on the row. He never spoke. So why give him a hard time? So what if a drop dead double for Marilyn Monroe came just to see him? There were tons of these babes who fell in love with killers, left their husbands and their kids and shit, for what? It was just one of those sicko realities a decent guy had to get used to.

The shoe man trudged silently beside the guard, who stood to his right. The shoe man allowed the guard to comb his fingertips through his wiry hair as Raphael hovered over his left shoulder. The guard buttoned his top shirt button and straightened his tie.

When the guard said, "We want to be pretty,"

Jack said, "Thank you very much, Willy. We want you to know we never killed a soul," and that was all he said.

The shoe man let himself be led into the visitors' cage. And because mortal words meant so little to him that the words Willy had said about the woman went no deeper than his ears, he looked up, expecting to see his unwelcome lawyer.

A cluster of guards ogled Lucille from just outside the wire as Buddy stood at her side. "Jack!" she cried, reaching her arms through the air toward the shoe man's shape for an embrace and missing. The shoe man ducked and howled his misery. Who was this? With him. Who was she? With him. His angels commanded caution. Beware, they said, beware of Lilith, beware of Eve, beware of Angela, of woman. This woman, not quite his Lucille, not quite his angel, not the same, was with him. A trap. It was a trap. The devil. He would not yield. Raphael gave him strength. Gabriel gave him courage. "Get away!" he hissed. Buddy Lomax grinned. He'd expected as much. The shoe man pounded the wire. "Get me out!" he screamed. "Out!" He pushed his whole body into the metal as if he could squeeze his skin through the mesh to the other side. He tore at his face with his nails. "They're mine! You won't have them! Get out!"

The guards apologized to Lucille as Buddy held her weeping against his heart.

"He's never been like that before," said Willy.

"Oh, Jack," she sobbed. "My Jack. Poor Jack." And then, tearing herself from Buddy so violently she ripped his silk shirt, she spat, "It's you." She ran down the prison corridor, stumbling toward light only to find more shadow.

Buddy shrugged at the gaping guards and ran after her. He caught her. She let him catch her. She had no choice. Where could she go? She couldn't see. But she saw now what she'd failed to see with all the sight she'd had and never used in her sad short muddled life. There was that to be grateful for, in a way. But she wasn't, and she didn't think of life as being long and time as being something she still had quite a lot of. She was more afraid than she'd ever ever been and that was all she knew she knew. "What the hell have you done?" she asked her captor. He was her captor. She knew that now. "What are you going to do?"

f only Buddy had answered her, summed up his plan and confessed his deeds the way the guilty always do on hour-long television mysteries and then shot her, he might have been caught. Put away. Not that that would have saved the shoe man or exposed the boyish killers of the mass murderer. But it would have been satisfying, wouldn't it, to see him get his comeuppance?

And if only Lucille had survived his shot, well, who knows? Though she might never have recovered full sight, she might have recovered from Buddy Lomax and his wickedness. Not right away, of course, but eventually. First she would have had to find her way back to what there was of herself and then make something other than a dead movie star out of what she had.

Ah, if only.

As you know, we must put if only in a bottle and throw it to sea in the hope that someone else will pick it up. It is of no use to us.

Buddy tormented Lucille with his silence. He poured her a vodka as he removed all evidence that might, in any way, connect him with her unhappiness. The Marilyn books, he kept. An interest was an interest. No one could blame him for that. They might actually be useful to explain his connection with the shoe man. How else would he have known about the angels before anyone else?

Buddy unplugged the telephone at the jack, handed her the TV remote control and left a bottle of vodka, a bottle of diazepam and a bottle of nitrazepam directly in front of the lamp on his night table where she would be able to see them silhouetted.

He loaded his Nikon with high-speed film and kissed his Marilyn goodbye. She bit his tongue. He resisted the urge to slap her. His hand might leave a mark. In the movie in his head, this was a moment for words. But Buddy couldn't think of anything for the history books, so he unzipped his pants and had Miss Marilyn Monroe one last hungry hard powerful time.

She clung to him, to her known enemy. What could she do? She had no friends. "Take me with you," she pleaded.

"Sorry, honey," he answered. "Where I'm going you can't go, and where you're going I can't follow." That wasn't too bad, he thought, though he'd never repeat it to the police.

"What the hell d'you mean by that?" she snapped, groping on the bed for a robe to wrap around her body. She saw his shadow leave the room and heard the door close and lock. "You're supposed to love me!" she shrieked, but she knew he was gone and she was alone with the TV. Moving shadows. Didn't listen. Didn't care. They just kept talking. And then they stopped. In-in-ugh-burp-indigestion. Come in now for Dodge Clearance Days. What did you bring home? Diarrhea. She threw the remote control at the screen, hoping to shatter the glass. But it bounced off the surface, which wasn't glass, it was durable plastic, and now the remote control was lost, somewhere, in the dark, on the floor and the TV kept talking talking talking and why had Jack gone crazy? What had she done? If she'd never met him, if she'd left him alone, if she'd only taken her shoes somewhere else or had a job in the plant back home. Poor Jack. Poor, poor Jack. Light shined prettily through the lemon vodka. It made a star with moving points. She reached for it and toppled the pills. Why not? Who cared? They stopped the pain. She sang with the TV. She knew the jingles. Drink Big Bob's. So cool it's hot. "That's me," she said to herself. "That used to be me. Before

I was perfect." She raised the bottle and toasted her shadow and raised the pill vial and swallowed down. "Ooh!" The more pills the more cure. The more cure, the better, the merrier, the happily ever after and screw Buddy in a big way. Let him find another Marilyn as good as her. Let him try. She was the one who was Marilyn. Not him. Who was he? He didn't love her. God would love her. He loved everybody. Even her. He had to. It was his job.

leven P.M. The TV was talk talk talking. A man's voice. And then the song. "We're all connected. New York Telephone." And then a woman. And an image Lucille couldn't have seen.

Live from the deserted city courthouse. A tiny folded-over man holding tight to a stair rail, buried his face in the enveloping bulk of a dark-skinned woman wearing a fur coat and a flowered kerchief.

"No comment. No comment," the woman said in a melodic foreign voice. "Leave us in peace." This, Lucille might have heard.

The reporter backed away. She knew the story without

her comment. The angel thief was freed on bail into the custody of an unnamed friend.

Theft charges had been dropped until further notice. "These angels, these extraordinary angels . . ." the reporter said. The scholars from Bavaria, Avignon and Rome agreed on what they weren't.

The angels weren't Renaissance.

The angels weren't Baroque.

They weren't quatrocento.

They weren't even old.

They weren't European.

And they weren't stolen.

They possessed the vitality of the Eros by Peter Vischer the Younger and vividness of Blake in three passionate dimensions. Some were half-eyed, with an unworldly mysticism most similar to the painter Raphael's Disputa del Sacramento. Others had a wide open gaze that said, Yes, yes, Here I am, Believe in me, in a frank, Hi, how ya doin', no-nonsense American way. And they provoked in these experts, who had never seen angels in life, but only in art, a yearning to know. It was as if they beheld the purest emotion, love, embodied in wood, as if irresistible, transforming love had carved them as close to life as they could come without the holy spark.

What they were . . . was a miracle.

And it seemed, although it was hard to place this man and his hands and his face and his job and his place and his time and his troubled soul in league with greatness, it seemed that the shoe man himself had been the Angel Carver. Either the shoe man or, as the reporter skeptically observed, the dead Heinz. But the Angel Carver's tools, burnishers, knives, brushes, et cetera, had been found in the shoe man's oven. The gold leaf was sold in Bensonhurst, and the supplier remembered his face. A Hasidic Brooklyn Jew came forward to claim that he, and before him his father, had personally sold the proprietor of Reliable Repair all the sapphires, diamonds, rubies, emeralds, opals and topaz to be found in the angels' eyes and he had the paperwork to prove it.

No one had known. Not his landlady. Not the Koreans or the Albanians or the Haitians or the Russians or the Yemenites. Not Gloria the pizza lady. No one. Did Lucille hear this or not?

Did she hear the reporter add that these alleged revelations didn't necessarily mean he wasn't also a murderer, an *alleged* murderer?

The shoe man's court appointed lawyer alleged that the angle of bullet entry didn't match the alleged angle of fire on the videotape, that even if the shoe man had allegedly fired, he couldn't have killed the mass murderer, and that the shoe man owned a crappy bodega popgun, not an automatic rifle.

Nobody bought his argument, but the judge agreed there

wasn't enough to indict. Not yet. Possession of a firearm was a dime a dozen crime, and without the counts of theft there wasn't enough to keep him locked up. As far as the press was concerned, he was free.

Lucille was found on the bed, naked and dead, dead with her hand on the telephone. What do you think? Had she heard the news of the shoe man's salvation and tried to save herself?

Lucille was found. Marilyn in life, she was Marilyn in death, and it was the perfection of her still white body that made the building superintendant shiver. He'd seen death before, but none so exquisite.

And how was it the super saw her first?

Buddy came to him at 5 A.M., confessing he'd worked until dawn at The Agency, pounding the Hell to meet a deadline. (Signed in. Signed out. And the guard saw him there. Buddy was a devil but never a fool.) In his exhaustion, he said, and his hurry to get home, he'd lost his keys.

Who else could let him in?

He wept. The super wasn't surprised at that. Buddy wailed, said they'd quarreled, yes, a lovers' spat, a few words, but how was he to know?

To the super it seemed strange and cold that a man should raise a camera to his eye and photograph the awful scene of his lover's death at its discovery, strange and cold, until Buddy said, "The police will want to investigate."

Then it made some kind of horrible sense.

But the police didn't want to investigate much, not before breakfast near a shift change. It was suicide. That was plain. And though she was a dead ringer, Marilyn had died in 1962. There weren't any presidents or ball players or genius playwrights involved. Just a shoe man, an Angel Carver.

And Buddy saw no reason to mention that. Yet.

THE ANGEL CARVER

ot knowing where else to go that night,
Leopoldine took the shoe man home to Parker
Street. He ran down the hall to the back room. The room
was empty but for the couch. The angels were gone. He
wasn't alarmed. They were with him. They were safe in his
mind.

With a gracious smile, he turned to Leopoldine. "Leopoldine," he said, as if she'd just come through the jingling door
of Reliable Repair. "What brings you to town?"

"Now, don't you be asking me too many questions this
hour of night," she answered. "Let's get to bed." She undressed him and bathed him, smacked the pillows full of air
and tucked him under the blankets with a kiss on his fore-

head. "Nighty night, sleep tight, and don't let those bedbugs bite."

The shoe man did as he was told.

Leopoldine awakened him before sunrise, put a hat on his head and bustled him into the Black Pearl cab that was waiting for them at the curb. The cab took them to Kennedy Airport, where Leopoldine had time to buy them both coffee and chocolate croissants before they took the shuttle bus to Newark. Leopoldine did not intend to be caught.

By the time news crews swarmed up Parker Street, humming and buzzing and hoping to surround and question the great Angel Carver himself, the shoe man and Leopoldine were in the air on their way to the Bahamas.

The shoe man had never flown before, except in his dreams. And here he was in the clouds. Through white, through blue, through rainbows they flew, and the shoe man was happy, pressing his face against the window to see the light spilling out of the sky and bouncing across the sea. Leopoldine held his hand.

They landed at Nassau. Leopoldine asked if he'd like to sight-see for an hour. The shoe man wanted nothing but to be back up in the heavens. And so he was, soon enough.

Leopoldine and the shoe man were traced to Eleuthera. Beyond that, there were no clues.

Need I say the angels were on their side?

THE ANGELS

The angels flew beside the small four-seater plane from island to island until the shoe man and Leopoldine reached the island of her birth. They stayed near to him, assuring him when he felt the old heat of fear. They protected him as he slept, tired at the end of every endless day, too tired for dreams, too satisfied to want. Leopoldine saw to that. Jack, no one on the island knew him as anything but Jack, Leopoldine's cherished friend, slept well with his belly against Leopoldine's warm back in a featherbed by an open window overlooking the sea.

The angels walked with him as he walked, feeling the sand under his bare feet, eating fresh black striped figs and fat mangoes to the pit.

One day he forgot them.

After strong morning coffee, there were chickens to feed and goats to tend. Fences always needed repair and when the fences were done, joints needed grease, when the joints were greased, there was painting to be done. The bright sun bleached the colors pale in no time, and when the sun was down, there was rum to drink and cake to eat and songs to sing with his new love before they rolled in her bed, new songs, new friends, no past that mattered here, no use for memories. What he lived was what there was and no one on the island owned a working camera.

Amen.

ABOUT THE AUTHOR

Rosanne Daryl Thomas is a graduate
of the Columbia University film school, and
the author, under the pseudonym Prince Charming,
of *Complications.* She lives in
Ridgefield, Connecticut.

ABOUT THE TYPE

This book was set in Bodoni, a typeface
designed by Giambattista Bodoni (1740–1813), the
renowned Italian printer and type designer.
Bodoni originally based his letterforms
on those of the Frenchman Fournier, and created
his type to have beautiful contrasts
between light and dark.